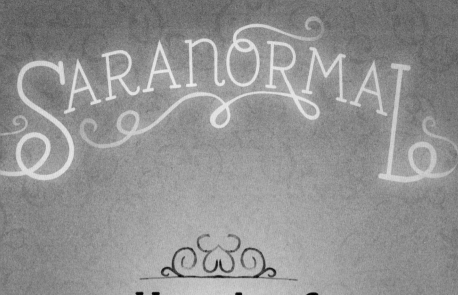

SARANORMAL

Mischief
Night

by Phoebe Rivers

SIMON SPOTLIGHT

New York London Toronto Sydney New Delhi

This book is a work of fiction. Any references to historical events, real people, or real locales are used fictitiously. Other names, characters, places, and incidents are the product of the author's imagination, and any resemblance to actual events or locales or persons, living or dead, is entirely coincidental.

SIMON SPOTLIGHT
An imprint of Simon & Schuster Children's Publishing Division
1230 Avenue of the Americas, New York, New York 10020
Copyright © 2012 by Simon & Schuster, Inc.
All rights reserved, including the right of reproduction in whole or in part in any form.
SIMON SPOTLIGHT and colophon are registered trademarks of Simon & Schuster, Inc.
Text by Heather Alexander
For information about special discounts for bulk purchases, please contact Simon & Schuster Special
Sales at 1-866-506-1949 or business@simonandschuster.com.
Manufactured in the United States of America 0712 FFG
First Edition 10 9 8 7 6 5 4 3 2 1
ISBN 978-1-4424-5221-3 (pbk)
ISBN 978-1-4424-5380-7 (hc)
ISBN 978-1-4424-5222-0 (eBook)
Library of Congress Catalog Card Number 2012934011

Chapter 1

Everything changes so fast.

Yesterday the rides and game stands were all open. The thump of repeating bass lines from the concert on the pier could be heard as far away as the lighthouse. Thousands of people milled about. Laughing. Shouting.

Today the boardwalk stood eerily quiet.

No music. No giggling toddlers. No guys haggling you to throw a softball at a milk bottle. Only a few screaming seagulls broke through the Sunday afternoon silence.

Summer in Stellamar was now officially over. Not officially in the calendar sense. That happened last month. Over, according to the boardwalk—and here in Stellamar, the boardwalk is everything. Last night was the annual October Boardwalk Bash, a town-wide good-bye party to the tourists, the lazy days in the sun, the ever-present carnival.

I lingered inside the doorway of the arcade and peered out at the now-shuttered stands and frozen Ferris wheel. Only the arcade, the pizza place, the ice-cream place, and a hot dog stand or two braved the change of season. Heavy steel-colored clouds crept down to meet the dark waters of the Atlantic. The sand below the boardwalk's graying wood looked bleak— the colorful kaleidoscope of towels and umbrellas already a memory. The humidity had lifted, blown away along with the scents of cotton candy, popcorn, and grilled sausage and peppers.

Change was in the air.

Not a big deal for me. For the past three months, change was all I'd done. New town. New house. New school. New friends.

Lots of new.

Without the boardwalk, what would this New Jersey town be like? I wondered. I pulled my hands up into my sweatshirt sleeves. When summer came around again, would I be one of the group? A local?

Would that ever happen? Or would I still be the quiet blond girl from California?

"Hey, Sara. Come play this!" Lily Randazzo called from inside the arcade.

My new friend.

Some new was good, I decided as I walked into the warm, yellow glow of the arcade. Lily's smile rivaled the bright video game lights. *Maybe I can really fit in here,* I thought. Lily waited by the skee-ball lanes with Miranda Rich and Avery Apolito.

"Let's see who can get the highest score," Miranda challenged us. Miranda liked to turn everything into a competition.

"I want to take home that pink bear." Avery pointed to an enormous fuzzy animal that resembled a fat dog more than a bear. Avery was one of the shortest girls in the seventh grade. The bear-dog, dangling on a hook from the wood-beamed ceiling, looked larger than her.

"There's no way." Lily twirled a strand of her long, dark hair around her finger, contemplating the prize. "It's too many tickets. You'd have to get every ball in the fifty slot for three games in a row. Try for that stuffed baseball with a face. It's only fifty tickets."

Avery scrunched her freckle-covered nose. "I have five of those already. My dog won't even play with them." She glanced around the arcade. There were maybe ten of us in the whole place. All summer it had been packed, but now it was just us. "Come on, Lily. Can't you do something?" Avery asked.

"Not here, Ave. Mr. Chopra isn't family." Lily lowered her voice. "In fact, I think he secretly hates my family. Thinks there's too many of us."

"There *are* a lot of you," Miranda quipped.

"The more the merrier, my mom says," Lily shot back with a grin.

"Two's company, three's a crowd, *my* mom says," Miranda countered.

"But four's a party—and so is forty!" They both laughed. Even though I'd just moved here a few months ago, I'd heard this back-and-forth routine many times. Lily had more relatives living and working in Stellamar than the ocean had shells. They seemed to run everything, except, it turned out, the arcade.

"We could try to win it together," Lily suggested. "The four of us all play and do amazing and then pool our tickets together."

"I'm in." Miranda dropped her token into the slot. Ten wooden baseball-size balls rolled down the chute, knocking one another as they came to a stop in a line.

Lily, Avery, and I each claimed a lane and pushed in a token.

"I got it! Fifty points!" Miranda whooped.

"Seriously? Seriously? What is wrong with me?" Lily stamped her foot next to me. She'd already bowled two balls up the ramp. Zero points flashed on her scoreboard. "Ugh. I was so close to that hundred-point hole."

"That's only there to distract you. Just aim up the middle," Miranda called.

I let the weight of the smooth ball rest in my palm. *How many other twelve-year-olds have thrown this ball over the years?* I thought. Hundreds, probably. I swung my arm back, then followed through, twisting my wrist slightly the way my dad had taught me. The ball glided into the fifty-point slot.

I rolled the next ball in line. Another fifty.

This got Miranda's attention. "You're good," she said, her surprise obvious.

I shrugged as if it were a natural talent. But it

wasn't. Dad and I had spent many nights in the arcade when we had first moved here and didn't know anyone. He showed me how to put the right amount of spin on the little wooden ball.

"Go again!" Avery urged. "Maybe we can win the bear."

I rolled the next ball. Not enough spin. Twenty points.

Lily finished her game and turned to watch. Avery edged closer. I tried to concentrate. Think only about the ball. Empty my mind.

"You are so lame!"

"No, you are. Can't even walk."

"Get your foot out of my way."

I glanced toward the door. A group of boys from our school tumbled in, punching each other in the arms. I saw Jack L. and Luke. But there were others behind them. Was *he* with them?

I wanted to look. To find his warm brown eyes. His crooked smile. But then what? Nothing, I knew. It'd been a week since he'd even said hi to me in class.

So I focused on the skee-ball lane instead. Visualized the ball's path. In one swift motion, I rolled the wooden ball, watching it hop, then drop into the fifty slot.

"The Harvest Queen is lucky," a familiar voice said behind me.

"Not luck. Skill," I replied, not turning. Not looking at him.

He was here. Next to me.

I reached for another ball. Studied the scuffed ramp while inhaling the faint scent of almonds. I loved that smell. Hosten's soap. I knew that because I'd smelled all the soaps at the drugstore last week until I found the right one. Hosten's comes in a three-pack. It was Jayden's soap, I was sure.

Avery giggled. Jack said something to her I couldn't hear.

I tossed the ball. It veered far to the right. Zero points.

"Luck," he said again.

"You messed me up." I turned, pretending to be angry.

"I'm sorry, Your Royal Highness."

I cringed. "Don't call me that," I said. "That's over."
Two weeks ago, I was crowned Harvest Queen for the

school dance. Most of Stellamar Middle School seemed to have forgotten already, except for a few mean girls in the eighth grade who blamed me for ruining their quest to be even more popular than they already are. And Jayden. He brought it up almost every time he saw me. I think he just thought it was funny.

It was, I guess, if you really know me. The real me. The title, the wearing the crown at the dance, hey, even going to the dance, was so not me. I only did it to help someone. I never thought I'd win.

But does he know me that well? I wondered. There was still so much about Jayden Mendes I didn't know. Didn't understand.

"I have twenty more tokens. Let's take photos," Lily announced.

"Yes! Let's go!" Avery squealed. She grabbed my hand, tugging me across the arcade to the photo booth. I tripped along, guessing the bear-dog quest had been called off. Miranda followed too.

The four of us piled into the narrow booth. Miranda's long legs dangled outside the curtain, as she and Lily squeezed onto the metal bench. Avery and I perched on their laps, trying not to block their faces. Lily began giggling and couldn't stop. Her laughter was contagious. Avery started snorting.

The photo strip slid from the slot, revealing all of us doubled over with laughter. I looked ridiculous. We shot different combinations. Lily and Avery. Lily and Miranda. Lily and me. Lily had a thing for the photo booth. One wall in her bedroom was covered with hundreds of photo booth strips that she'd woven together. She's in every one, smiling broadly. That pretty much sums up Lily. The center of everything.

"Coming in!" Jack called. He and Luke barreled into the booth. Lily and Avery tried unsuccessfully to push them out.

Garrett and Jayden stood outside the booth. Garrett yanked the pale blue curtain closed. "Time to get cozy!"

Luke flailed his leg out and kicked Garrett in the shin. "Grow up, man!" He opened the curtain and they all tumbled out. Then Miranda and Jack took a photo, pretending to fight. Avery pulled Garrett into the booth next, both making monster faces.

"Our turn," Jayden said suddenly. He nudged me into the booth with his shoulder. I glanced at Lily, who wiggled her eyebrows at me. She knew I liked Jayden.

I slid across the metal bench until my right side pressed against the wall. For a moment, I sat in the little capsule alone. Waiting. Jayden seemed oddly frozen. Then, as if making up his mind about something, he stepped in and sat right beside me. Someone pulled the cotton curtain closed.

I had never been so close to him.

The sleeve of his black T-shirt touched my gray sweatshirt. I gulped. The sound from my throat seemed to echo loudly in our little metal box.

I bit my lip. Should I say something? What?

"Hey," he said softly, turning to look at me.

"Hey." I was too scared to look at him. I studied my navy high-tops. The right shoelace dragged on the corrugated metal floor.

"You need to move over."

"Huh?" If I moved my left hand an inch I would brush his hand. So close.

"Only half your head's in the frame. Look." He raised his hand to the monitor that showed our faces. My blond hair and blue eyes seemed so pale next to his caramel skin and thick brown hair.

I inched closer to him, praying he couldn't feel me

tremble. I tried to look natural, to smile. I wanted this photo to look good. The monitor counted down.

Ten . . . nine . . .

The air in our box grew warmer. Heavier. I could smell him. Almond soap. So close.

Eight . . .

But something else too. Something sour.

Seven . . . six . . .

Hot. So hot. The rotten smell clung to my nose and crept along the back of my throat. I needed fresh air.

Five . . .

Where was Jayden? My vision blurred. I could no longer sense his body next to me. It was as if someone had wedged a board between us. I struggled to turn my head. The air felt as thick as mud.

Four . . . three . . .

Jayden. He was still here. But there was someone between us.

Someone I recognized.

Someone who sent a chill down my spine.

I pressed my palms into my jeans, wanting to scream. Knowing I couldn't.

We weren't alone.

Two . . .

Jayden's older brother.

He'd been dead for seven years.

Dead.

But I could see him. Smell him. Feel him.

Dead. But here with us.

I have this weird bond with the dead that none of my friends know about. I can't tell them about it. Can't let them know. So I couldn't scream. I had to hold it in.

Lily couldn't know I saw spirits.

Jayden couldn't know Marco was here with us.

One . . .

The camera clicked. The flash illuminated the booth as the force of Marco's spirit shoved me. With nowhere to go but into the wall, I doubled over. The raised diamond pattern on the floor danced before me.

The curtain yanked open. Lily's smiling face pushed in. "Let me see the—" She stopped when she caught sight of me. "Are you okay?"

I raised my head slowly, still dizzy. Jayden eyed me, confused. The faint outline of his dead brother now stood outside the curtain. Arms crossed. Dark hoodie. Shorts. Glaring eyes. Challenging me.

"I'm fine," I mumbled. "It's kind of hot in here, that's all." I watched Lily studying me. "I forgot to eat lunch," I added.

"My mom usually has granola bars with her," she offered.

"Maybe later."

With another searching look, Lily let it go. Pulling the photo strip from the slot, she inspected it with a practiced gaze. "That's strange. Something must've gone wrong."

Jayden peered over her shoulder. "Yeah. Maybe the camera's broken." He handed me the flimsy strip of four photos.

In every square, I was completely blurred. Jayden looked fine. Smiling. Cute as always. I came out as a smudge.

As if I didn't belong next to him.

I held the strip in my shaking hands. The camera wasn't broken, I was sure of that. I knew what had happened. Jayden's dead older brother wanted me out of the picture.

Permanently.

Chapter 2

My fingertips fiddled with the photo strip I'd tucked into my sweatshirt pocket. Lily and I walked down Beach Drive, heading home.

I wouldn't throw it out, I decided. Throwing it out would be like giving in. Like letting Marco win. But win what?

Ever since I'd first met Jayden in science class, Marco had been forever by his side. Jayden had no idea.

And I had no idea why Marco's spirit was trying so hard to keep me and his brother apart. Why he hated me so much.

"Do you think Jayden likes me?" I asked Lily. I tried to sound as if it were just a random thought. That I hadn't spent weeks turning the question over and over in my mind.

"Hmm. Jack likes Avery for sure, but Jayden's kind of closed off. I think he likes you. But he's hard to figure out, you know?"

I did.

The sun pushed through the clouds. The store windows on the town's main street glittered with Halloween decorations. I fidgeted with the neck of my sweatshirt.

"I like that necklace," Lily said.

"I knew you would." Lily loved accessories. Even now, on a random Sunday, she wore several bangle bracelets, hoop earrings with tiny moveable beads, and a long, gauzy scarf. The necklace was the only jewelry I wore, besides the braided silver ring I wore on my middle finger.

I'd had the ring since I was a baby. It'd been my mom's.

The necklace was new.

Lily stopped to inspect it. "You wore this to the dance, right? But then it only had the one red crystal. Is the other one new? Do you collect them or something?"

I slid the crystals along the simple black cord. "Lady Azura gave them to me."

"I knew it!" Lily bounced on her toes. "If she gave them to you, they must mean something. Do they have powers?"

"She said they do." I touched the stones. Both were warm. They always radiated a faint heat. "The aquamarine is supposed to give me courage. The ruby crystal is to encourage love." I snorted. "That one must be defective."

"No way! They're going to work if she gave them to you. Jayden will fall in love with you. I know it!" Lily rubbed the stone, as if she could absorb its powers. "I want one too. Do you think she'll give me one?"

"Maybe. But who do you want to fall in love with you?"

We started walking again, turning onto Ocean Grove Road. I kicked the yellow pebbles overflowing from a driveway.

"I don't know. A cute boy. A cute boy I don't know yet."

I fiddled with the ruby crystal around my neck. Red flicks of light bounced against a white mailbox as it caught the sun. Did it really work? I wondered. I certainly wasn't very brave in that photo booth. I didn't even talk to Jayden. And then his brother . . .

I kicked another pebble and watched it skitter along the pavement. Lady Azura was the only person who knew I could communicate with the dead. She knew because she could do it too. Kind of. She'd gotten old and her abilities, or whatever you called them, were weak. But she knew about me, and we had even talked about it a little.

But she didn't know how much the spirits scared me. The helpless feeling I got that they were in control. If she did, she'd have given me more than one little crystal for courage. I needed a crystal mountain.

"Let's go visit Lady Azura," Lily suggested as we turned onto our street.

Lady Azura. To Lily, she was just a kooky woman who told fortunes and passed out crystals. But she was more than that. Much more. She knew things about the dead and the living. I sensed she had secrets and stories and important knowledge about how the universe worked.

Until we moved here, I hadn't wanted to know anything about the dead. I just wanted them to stay away from me.

But now . . . well, things were changing. Maybe I'd ask Lady Azura to share her secrets with me. In the few months since we'd arrived, I'd gone from avoiding her as much as possible to actually enjoying spending time with her. Most of the time, anyway. Sometimes she was still just too weird to deal with.

We passed Lily's house and headed two doors down. With its gabled windows and octagonal turret, our old Victorian looked like an illustration in a fairy-tale book. All the houses on our street had that Hansel-and-Gretel gingerbread design. Ours just looked more run-down. Peeling yellow paint. Splintered shingles. Browning leaves blanketing the yard.

It wasn't ours, though. Lady Azura owned it. We rented the top two floors. She lived and worked on the ground floor. I still couldn't figure out why my dad chose for us to move here rather than one of the new town houses by the beach. It was a lot of house for just the two of us. Three of us with Lady Azura.

I climbed the wide wooden steps to the wraparound porch and stared at the two pale elderly figures, side by side on the double porch swing. One woman, gray hair pinned in a loose bun, focused her lifeless gaze on her clacking knitting needles. The other old woman, her face similarly lined with wrinkles, flipped the pages of *Vogue* magazine. The muted hue of her camel shift dress with the wide bell sleeves emphasized her crimson lipstick and jet-black mascaraed lashes. Her eyes flashed with intensity.

Of course, Lady Azura was alive. The woman with the bun next to her had been dead for decades. Her shimmery spirit would sit forever on the porch swing, knitting a scarf that had no end. There . . . but not there.

"Girls!" Lady Azura cried, urgency in her raspy voice. "What do you think about polka dots?"

"Love 'em," Lily said, skipping to her side. She gazed at the magazine Lady Azura held open. A beautiful model wore a speckled coat with a high collar. "Oh, but not those tiny dots. Too dizzying. I like my dots bigger," Lily pronounced.

"I agree. Let life be your pattern, I say." Lady Azura closed the magazine and rested it on her bony knees.

I thought the coat was kind of pretty, but I didn't offer my opinion. Lily and Lady Azura lived and breathed fashion and could probably spend hours talking about clothes and accessories. But not me.

"What's new?" Lily asked, walking in front of Lady Azura as if to sit next to her. But in doing so, she would be sitting right on top of the knitting spirit!

Lady Azura's arthritic hand with its long, oval-shaped nails reached for Lily's shoulder and gently, but firmly, guided her to the floor. "Sit down here where I can see you," she said. She caught my eye, knowing that I, too, saw that the swing was otherwise occupied. What a strange secret to share.

I knelt next to Lily, looking up at Lady Azura.

"New . . . something new, you asked." Lady Azura pondered Lily's question. She gazed over her shoulder at the wooden sign in the large bay window: LADY AZURA: PSYCHIC, HEALER, MYSTIC.

In the afternoon sun, the dark purple lettering looked tired and worn. And for the first time since my dad and I had moved into her house, I thought Lady Azura looked tired as well. I knew she was really old— probably in her eighties, according to my dad. Most days, she matched my energy. But not today.

"Nothing is new," she said. "It's been a strange fall. I usually get a lot of business this time of year. But here I sit alone. No one interested in knowing what the future holds. I suspect the cause to be an odd planetary alignment."

"What does that mean?" I asked.

"When two planets form an angle with the sun in the middle, it's not a good time for any business." She shrugged her thin shoulders. "And that's not good for my piggy bank."

"If people's businesses are bad, then they should definitely see you to find out what's coming next. To plan for their future," Lily said. "You could read their palms or tea leaves."

"I agree," Lady Azura said. "My art, and it is an art, does have a practical side. But it is a different world today, girls. People no longer look within for answers. They want to press a button on their phones and have the answers sent to them. But from whom? I ask. From where?"

"If people knew how cool you were, they'd come to you," Lily said loyally. She was a true, devoted follower since she'd gotten to know Lady Azura.

"Thank you, my dear. But they are not coming. Not at all. My tarot cards are dusty."

"Halloween is almost here," I said. "I'm sure people will want to get their fortunes told then."

"Yes! Halloween!" Lily cried. "You'll have lots of customers then."

"Clients. They are clients," Lady Azura corrected her. "And I fear that is not in the cards for me. Not this year."

"Well, then you need a new deck of cards," Lily declared.

I smiled. Lily never thought there was a problem she couldn't fix.

"You need to advertise," she continued. "My dad manages all these strip malls. When a business leaves, my dad can't have an empty store, 'cause he says an empty store doesn't make any money. So he posts ads to get new stores to take the space. Even my aunt Dolores puts up ads to get new people to buy the clothes in her store, the Salty Crab. That's the one on Beach Drive with the dresses that look like tablecloths. Ugly, but lots of women go in there." Lily stood, excited by her speech. "Advertising! That's what you need."

Lady Azura swung gently back and forth on the swing. "It's like a dog chasing his tail. Advertising may bring in money, but it costs money. And money I don't have."

"I could make you flyers," I offered. She'd been trying to help me since I'd moved in. I suddenly realized I wanted to help her. "Really graphic ones that people would notice. We could even post your ad to some websites that don't cost money."

"Totally," Lily agreed. "It can be like a pre-Halloween special. Uncle Lenny does that at his pizzeria for holidays . . . half-price pies to celebrate the holidays or whatever. You could do half-price readings for the rest of October to celebrate Halloween!"

"You girls can really do all that?" Lady Azura asked.

"Of course we can! Sara's great on the computer. It'll be fun. We'll start now," Lily said, talking a mile a minute. "We'll get so many people coming in and out of this house you'll need a second crystal ball. Or an assistant. Hey, I could so be that. Your fortune-telling room is so amazing."

"Thank you, Lily. But I do more than gaze into a crystal ball, you know." An amused smile played across Lady Azura's dark-red lips.

"Oh, I know." Lily nudged me up from the porch.

"Sara, in the ad, wouldn't it be cool if we say that this house is haunted?"

"*Haunted?*" I blurted out loudly before I could stop myself. I bit my lip and tried not to stare at the shimmery gray figure on the swing. Knitting. *Haunting.*

"Yeah. That there are ghosts here, brought back from the dead by Lady Azura's powers. That would totally bring kids here. Adults too." Lily pushed her oversize sunglasses up onto her dark hair. Her brown eyes glinted with excitement.

"But that's not what we're advertising. I mean, it's supposed to be fortune-telling." I could hear the tightness in my voice. "We can't just make things up."

"We're not *lying*. We're setting the scene," Lily said. "Besides, who's to say it's not true, right? Maybe there are ghosts in this house."

"Maybe there are," Lady Azura said breezily. "What do you think, Sara?"

My gaze wandered up to the second-floor windows. Spirits lurked behind the white curtains. Dead men, women, and children. They lived among us. Here. At school. At the arcade. Everywhere.

But they were a secret. My secret. I glared at Lady Azura. *Our secret.*

Lily couldn't know. She might tell Miranda, and Miranda would tell the whole school. I'd be called weird. Abnormal.

"There are no ghosts," I said firmly.

Chapter 3

"Do you hear that?" Lily asked.

"What?" I wiggled the mouse, trying to position the crystal-ball clip art around the text. Lady Azura's flyer filled the oversize computer monitor in my craft room. It hadn't taken too long to design.

Lily perched on the edge of a huge yellow table. "Listen," she whispered.

I stopped and listened. Autumn leaves on the maple tree outside the window rustled slightly against the house. "What did you hear?"

"I'm not sure," Lily admitted. "A banging noise, I think." Her eyes darted around the large third-floor room. Stacks of my crafting materials covered the table and lay piled in the corners. My dad had strung old Christmas lights around the window for me, framing the view out over the bay. The tiny white bulbs blinked on and off.

I shrugged. "This big old house always makes noise. I put this photo I took of Lady Azura on the flyer. Okay? I added a mystical aura around it."

"Definitely." Lily's shoulders relaxed, and she flipped through a stack of colored paper. "Let's print them on this sparkly paper." She fed a stack into my printer.

I love my craft room. My dad created it for me as a surprise right after we moved here. I think he knew I was bummed out about moving, and he did it to cheer me up. My dad is amazing like that.

The only other room up here on the third floor is empty, still coated with the dust of the last decade. Dad and I can't even find a way to use all the rooms on the second floor, where our bedrooms and family room are. He worries, though. He thinks I spend too much time up here alone, fiddling around on Photoshop and making frames and trays with the shells I collect on the beach.

Thump.

That time I heard it too. The sound came from the closet in the far corner. A closet I hadn't opened since we moved in. A closet that should be empty.

Thump. Thump.

"You heard that, right?" Lily whispered, her eyes wide.

I licked my lips, stalling.

Thump.

I wanted to pretend I hadn't heard anything. That we truly were alone.

"It's coming from that closet!" Lily scooted toward my desk. "Sara, what's in that closet?"

I gritted my teeth, willing my eyes away from the closet door. Willing the noise to stop.

"I don't know," I said softly. I didn't know.

But I had an idea.

A bad idea.

"Maybe we should show Lady Azura how it looks so far," I suggested, trying desperately to change the subject. I clicked print. *I have to get Lily out of here,* I thought.

The printer whirred to life, its motor unable to mask the *thump, thump, thump* from the closet door.

"We can't just sit here!" Lily whispered. Panic laced her voice.

"So let's go downstairs," I urged. I stood, but Lily was faster. She lunged across the room, her hand twisting the tarnished brass knob of the closet.

"Lily, no! Wait—"

But Lily didn't wait.

She pulled at the doorknob. It didn't open. She pulled again. The hinges stuck.

"Lily, stop!"

The door finally flew open. Lily dropped to the floor, her hands protecting her head from—

Nothing. Darkness. Silence.

Lily stood. I tiptoed beside her. Together we peered into the closet. Two wire hangers dangled on a wooden rod.

"Sara," Lily whispered faintly. She pointed to the hangers. "They're moving."

I stared at the hangers. They were swaying.

The windows were closed. No breeze. Something had moved the hangers.

Something, or more likely . . . someone.

My heart beat rapidly.

"It—it was the force of—of opening the door." I fumbled for an explanation. "Totally our imaginations making us freak out over nothing." I smiled and tried to look completely calm.

Lily nodded and backed away from the open closet.

"Let's go downstairs," I suggested again. "My dad already stocked up on Halloween candy for the trick-or-treaters, and I say we go raid it!"

But Lily wasn't listening. She scanned the room. "That was so freaky!" She seemed to be calming down, though. "That was like some hidden camera reality show."

I let out the breath I'd been holding. "Exactly."

Lily returned to the big table. She flicked on my iPod. The upbeat tune of the newest pop hit blasted through the small speakers, filling the room.

"I bet it was a mouse. We have them in our attic a lot," Lily said. "Or even a squirrel."

"Definitely." I inspected the flyer from the printer. It looked good. Professional. I didn't want to think about the closet. I printed twenty more. "We should link this onto the school site."

"We need Principal Bowman's okay." Lily held the stack and lifted up the flyer on top, reading it through. Her eyes, thankfully, were on the paper.

Not on the floor.

I watched in horror as a spool of ribbon rolled along the floor. Then another. Careening toward Lily.

My rolls of ribbon were no longer in a neat pile. One after another, they rolled across the floor.

I jumped toward them. My foot kicked the ribbon aside, as a glass jar of colorful buttons mysteriously tipped over. Buttons skittered crazily along the floor.

"What the—?" Lily started.

"Oh, I'm so clumsy," I said, pretending to trip. *Let her think I spilled them,* I prayed. *Please.*

"But—"

A container of glue dropped from the short book-case. The top mysteriously loosened, and a thick white puddle blossomed.

"Wow, everything's . . . um . . ." I moved toward the bookcase as a handful of paintbrushes bounced to the ground.

Focus, I urged myself. *Focus.* I stared at the book-case. *Focus!*

A glimmer. Something. A shape.

A box of markers clattered to the floor.

I narrowed my gaze. No blinking. Drawing it out. Toward me.

A hand. A small hand shimmered into view.

It grabbed the plastic tub of glitter. Twisted the top. Raised it. High. Higher.

"Lily!" I whirled about and grabbed her arm, my fingers pressing into her flesh. "Let's get out of here!" I pulled her out of the room and down the narrow stairs. Down. Down two flights, through the red foyer and out the front door. Onto the porch. Away.

We stood side by side, panting.

"Sara! Your house is haunted!" Lily was panting so hard she could barely get the words out. She clutched the stack of flyers to her chest.

My mind twisted in circles. I had to say something. But what? What could I say?

"Of course it is."

We both spun around. Lady Azura sat on the swing. The knitting woman was still beside her, unseen by Lily.

"I was just trying out some scares for my Halloween party. I have a party every year, you know." Lady Azura smiled reassuringly at Lily. "Sara's dad rigged everything up for me up there. I take it from the looks on your faces that it's all working as it should be?"

For a moment, I actually believed her. For a moment, I thought maybe my dad was in on it.

Then I caught Lady Azura's eye.

Saw her wink. At me.

"Oh, wow! You so got me!" Lily laughed, relief flowing through her. "Sara, were you in on it too?"

"Nope, it was a total surprise for me," I said. And that was technically the truth.

With that, Lily said good-bye and promised to text me later. She had to get home and help babysit.

I wanted to hug Lady Azura as I watched Lily walk toward her house, the flyers tucked under her arm. Lady Azura had saved me.

What was happening on the third floor? I wondered. I'd never had a spirit *throw* things at me.

I turned to ask the questions multiplying in my mind, when Dad drove his car up and parked in front.

My questions would have to wait, because my dad didn't know.

He didn't know we lived with ghosts. He didn't know I could see them.

Lady Azura placed her veiny hand on mine. "Later," she said.

I nodded, as Dad climbed the porch steps. "Hey, kiddo. How's everything? All good here? I saw Lily leaving. Sorry I missed her. I'll have to catch up with her the next time she's over."

There's never going to be a next time, I thought. My heart was still beating unnaturally fast.

I'd lied to Lily. We *did* have ghosts in our house. But there was no way to tell her the truth. I bit my lip. Lily could never come over again.

Never.

Chapter 4

Will you get an A on the test, or a D?
Is someone crushing on you?
Will you make millions? Will you be famous?
Take a look into your future with Lady Azura!

Heads bowed together, two girls whispered in front of the flyer posted on the school's main bulletin board by the office.

"I wish I knew what they were saying." I slowed, forcing Lily to stop and circle back to me. She always darted through the hallways, leaving me scrambling to keep up.

"That's easy. They're wondering if they'll be invited to the big eighth-grade party on Mischief Night," Lily answered. "They want to know if the all-knowing Lady Azura knows."

"You can hear them?" The school hallways were so loud, I had trouble understanding the person next to me.

"No. But trust me, that's what every girl is thinking about."

"I'm not. And what is Mischief Night?" I didn't even know what Lily was talking about. I might have been crowned Harvest Queen, but I was still clueless about life in our school. I'd figured out my classes and teachers okay, but that was baby stuff. Who kids were friends with or who they hated or who they were friends with but secretly hated. What the cool activities, the cool clothing brands, and the cool parties were. That info was at a level I hadn't yet achieved. At my old school, I'd never been able to crack that code. Here, though, things were looking up. I'd actually made some friends.

But Lily had already moved on to the next subject. I'd have to ask about this party later.

"Just be really into it," Lily was saying. "Upbeat. Like you live for journalism." She stopped in front of a classroom. "Mrs. Notkin is kind of tough, but you'll like her."

I hesitated and peeked into the room. About thirty

kids filled the desks, staring up at a teacher with thick black hair twisted into a side braid. I slid into one of the last empty seats and watched the woman drum her fingers against her desk, staring impatiently at the clock on the wall.

At exactly three, she began the after-school meeting of the school's web newspaper, the *Stellamar Wire*. Lily had convinced me to join. She was a reporter. I had a plan for a different job. A plan that had started with Jayden.

I felt my face flush thinking about how he had smiled at me in science this morning. No words. Just a smile.

Right now, he was outside on one of the fields with the school soccer team. What position did he play? I had no idea. That was where my plan came in. I would become the newspaper's sports photographer. I'd go to the soccer games. I'd get to watch Jayden play. It would be totally normal, because watching him would be my *job*.

"Now, we'll divide into our groups to work on the different sections. I see some new faces today. New people, please come see me."

I jolted out of my Jayden dream. I'd missed most of what Mrs. Notkin had said.

"Good luck," Lily whispered before she headed off with a girl and a boy I didn't recognize.

I made my way to Mrs. Notkin's desk and waited while she talked to several other kids. I held a red folder in one hand.

"Hi," Mrs. Notkin said, her tone businesslike.

"Hi." Talking to adults made me nervous. I reached into my folder, pulled out the application sheet that Lily had me download from the *Wire* website, and thrust it toward her.

Mrs. Notkin scanned the paper. "A photographer. Good. Did you bring any work for me to see?"

I opened the folder, revealing three photographs that I'd blown up large. A swirly shell reflecting the glow of the setting sun. An overflowing trash can on the boardwalk. I'd taken that one just outside Midnight Manor this past summer. A worn, chipped gravestone in the little cemetery on the hill by the school. I'd visited that cemetery during the school dance a few weeks ago, after I was crowned Harvest Queen. And bumped into Jayden there.

I'd worked hard on these photos, before I even knew about the newspaper and came up with my plan to be the sports photographer. I'd been taking photos for years. Playing with light and contrast. Trying to get it right. Trying to get it like my mom did.

My mom was a photographer. She took the most beautiful photos of everyday things. I had three framed pictures hanging in my room at home. All were pictures of objects my mom had taken. My favorite one was a picture of a porcelain figurine in the shape of an angel.

I never knew her. She died giving birth to me, but looking at her photos makes me feel close to her. Like she's talking to me through the images.

Mrs. Notkin frowned. Obviously, my photos were not bringing about the same intense feelings for her.

"Do you have any action shots? Or ones with people?" she asked, sliding the images back into the folder.

"I don't usually photograph people," I admitted.

"Why not?"

How to explain? People were complicated. They were more than just a body and a story. They were made up of layers. Layers that sometimes got left behind after death.

A porcelain angel was just a porcelain angel.

I shrugged, staring down at my sneakers as if a better explanation were written there.

"I like your work, Sara," Mrs. Notkin said, smiling at me. "These pictures show a lot of talent. But a school newspaper is about people. People make the news. I have four other students who want to join us as photographer, but I have room for only two. I have asked them, as I will ask you, to bring me three samples of your best action photos or portraits of people. I will decide based on the merit of your work. Next week, bring me three new pictures, and we'll take it from there, okay?"

"Okay," I agreed. I was glad I hadn't told her I wanted to be the sports photographer. Not yet. First I had to prove myself.

I inhaled the smell of the cinnamon candles, as I fidgeted outside the purple velvet curtain. My camera hung by a strap off my shoulder. Voices murmured behind the curtain. Lady Azura's distinct rasp. A lower tone with a musical quality.

I smiled. She had a client. Maybe our flyers were working. Lily had plastered them everywhere her relatives worked—the pizza place, the ice-cream parlor, the motel, the visitors' center, and the clothing store. She'd pretty much covered the whole town.

A woman finally emerged. Skinny, in a pale pink polyester uniform that had ANCHOR MOTEL embroidered on an oversize pocket, she barely raised her eyes to me as she hurried out the front door.

"Her shift starts soon." Lady Azura poked her head out from the heavy curtain that divided her fortune-telling room and bedroom from the rest of the first floor. "You must thank Lily for me. I owe both of you girls thanks. That woman saw your advertisement."

"What did she want?"

Lady Azura shook her head. "I cannot reveal the content of my sessions. I am a professional." She turned back into the room.

I followed.

I snapped photos of her as she set everything back into place. Tarot cards straightened into a deck. Crystal ball shined with a soft yellow cloth, clearing the view into the future. Candles extinguished with a long-handled silver snuffer.

"Are you finished?" she asked. She was trying to pretend that my taking pictures of her was aggravating, but I knew better. I knew she liked it.

I didn't answer. I watched her through my viewfinder. She'd settled into the large armchair at the round center table. Her sapphire silk tunic contrasted with the nubby mustard-color fabric of the chair and made her look regal. She pressed her bony fingers together and stared back at me.

"Sara, stop hiding behind the camera," she commanded finally. "We should explore yesterday's . . . situation."

I slid onto the spindly wooden chair beside her and rested the camera in my lap. "Explore?"

"You know as well as I do there are spirits in this house."

"Of course I do," I snapped. I didn't mean to, but talking about ghosts put me on edge. I adjusted my tone. "I see and hear them all the time. That woman in the pink bedroom upstairs won't stop crying. And rocking. Her rocking chair is always squeaking." I leaned toward her. "But there's a spirit on the third floor too. He was there when Lily was over. She was really scared."

"I suspected that when I saw the two of you tumble out the front door. A bit melodramatic for you, Sara." She raised her eyebrows at me as if I had disappointed her.

"Maybe you're used to it. Dead people appearing. Talking to you. Getting in your face." My words spilled out. "But not me. I've been seeing them since I was little, but until I came into this house, they always left me alone. They didn't bother me. They didn't try to ruin my life!"

Lady Azura's eyes clouded with concern. "Wait. How are they ruining your life? What's happening, Sara?"

I took a deep breath. I hadn't been planning on telling her. But now it seemed like the right thing to do. "There's this spirit I've been seeing. He's always there. He follows this boy at school. He kind of watches over him. Makes everything easy for him. Clears a space at a crowded table or makes a path through the packed hallway." I ran my fingertip nervously over the delicate gold-lace overlay on the table. The silky red tablecloth peeked through the floral design. "This spirit . . . he doesn't like me. He *hates* me."

"What makes you say that?"

"He shoves me, pushes me, does anything he can to keep me away."

Lady Azura looked at me sharply. "He pushes you away from him?"

"No, away from the boy he guards, I think. He doesn't like it when I'm around for some reason." I raised my eyes to meet Lady Azura's. "I didn't do anything to him. I don't know why he's here."

"I suspect he's trapped," Lady Azura murmured, deep in thought.

"Trapped? Where?"

"Here, as opposed to wherever *there* is." She blinked her fake eyelashes rapidly. I'd noticed that she did that when she was thinking. "Every person has a soul. The soul is the essence of a person. The body is just a casing. An accessory, if you will. Death is not an end. When we die, our souls depart from our bodies, but there are times when souls simply can't move on."

"And so they stay behind, here on Earth . . ." I

finished hesitantly. "That's what I see. What *we* see."

Lady Azura nodded. "Exactly. They stay behind for many reasons. Revenge. Unfinished business. To warn someone. To protect someone. They remain until the deed is done." She sighed. "Sometimes, though, it is an impossible feat. An idea with no definite end. Then the souls become trapped, unable to move on, doomed to try and solve an unsolvable problem."

I pondered this. Jayden's brother, Marco, was trapped. He died and never left. But why?

"How can I find out why this spirit is still here?" I asked. "How do I get him to leave? To move on?"

"It's not your place to help him on his journey."

"What does that mean?" I cried in frustration. Lady Azura had a frustrating way of speaking in circles.

"It means that this spirit did not ask for your help. Alice asked you to become Harvest Queen. She came to you to help set her on her path. She came to you, so you could intervene. The spirit must always approach you."

"So I'm just supposed to let him push me around?" *And keep me away from Jayden,* I added silently.

"No. Not at all. In fact, you must tell the spirit to leave you alone. Command it." Her eyes blazed. "This is very important."

"But how do I make him leave for good? You know, go away and leave the boy he guards alone too?" She'd been communicating with the dead for almost a century. Surely she could tell me how to make him go away.

"Well, you could . . ." Her voice trailed off, and she shook her head. She'd changed her mind about whatever she'd been about to reveal. "Sara, I know it's hard, but you must mind your own business. Just stay away from this spirit. Stay away from the boy he follows." She looked me straight in the eyes. "Far away. Okay?"

I nodded but didn't hold her gaze. I knew it wasn't possible to stay away from Jayden. He was in my science class, after all.

Lady Azura suddenly pressed a pale lavender scrap of paper into my hand. I stared down at it. Had she changed her mind and written down for me how to get rid of Marco?

Whitening toothpaste
Fennel seed
Butterscotch Krimpets

Part of the deal my dad had made with Lady Azura to rent her house was that we'd help out. He'd do repairs. I'd run her errands after school. I sighed and shoved the list into my jeans pocket. I rode my bike down the street to Elber's, the convenience store on the corner.

I leaned into the handlebars and thought about Lady Azura. Why wouldn't she tell me what I needed to know? I'd seen her summon spirits for séances. I'd seen her look into the future. She'd even predicted that I'd meet Jayden at school this year and fall in love. Not by name, but it was him, and when school started, there he was. Waiting for me.

But Marco was waiting too.

I skidded to a stop in front of Elber's brick front and green-and-white awning. Wedging my bike next to a blue dirt bike on the rack, I entered the fluorescent glare of the store.

Mr. Elber raised his bushy eyebrows and leaned

his arms on the front counter. "Sara, I was wondering where you were. I thought maybe Lady Azura ran out of things to buy!"

"No chance of that," I teased. Lady Azura sent me to buy two or three things every day instead of doing one big shopping trip. Mr. Elber and I were becoming buddies.

I headed to the toothpaste aisle. I scanned all the choices for a sparkling smile, squatting to better reach the brand she liked. On to the next item. What was fennel seed? I wondered. Probably an herb or spice for her fortune-telling. I'd have to ask Mr. Elber.

Fortune-telling. If Lady Azura wouldn't tell me the secret to getting rid of a spirit, could she at least tell me what was going to happen next? Was I destined to spend the rest of the year dodging a teenage ghost?

"I see you," said an unnaturally deep and low voice.

I froze, my fingers still gripping the toothpaste box.

"I see you," the creepy voice murmured again.

Chapter 5

I glanced over my shoulder. Mr. Elber rearranged the display of lottery tickets by the counter. He didn't look alarmed. He hadn't heard anything.

I chewed my lip. Just me.

Slowly I stood up. I tried to ready myself for the spirit waiting for me. The spirit calling to me.

My eyes darted nervously up and down the aisle. Empty.

Then I saw the hair.

Thick wavy brown hair.

Hair I'd been staring at in class for weeks.

"I scared you." Jayden stepped out from behind the rack of chips.

Relief flooded me. I tried not to smile. "That wasn't funny."

"That's as funny as it gets at Elber's." He jerked his head in the direction of Mr. Elber furrowing his brows together as he attempted to color-code scratch-off cards. Was one color luckier than another?

I turned back to Jayden. He wore his gold-and-blue soccer uniform. Dirt was smeared on his left leg, from his thigh down to over his knee-high socks. Bits of grass clung to the caked mud.

"I guess you're buying soap," I teased, and immediately felt the color rise in my cheeks. Soap made me think about how last week I'd smelled all the soaps to figure out what made him smell like he did. I knew what brand he used. Suddenly my little comment was way too personal.

Jayden glanced at his leg. "Nah, this dirt is a badge of honor. I slid across the goal and bodily stopped the shot from going into it. I was the hero. This is my trophy. In fact"—he reached down and flecked off a small piece of dried mud—"I may sell it. For you, an excellent price!"

I rolled my eyes. "You wish. You'd have to pay *me*."

He grinned, then flicked the dirt at me.

I squealed.

Then I saw the shimmery figure in a dark hoodie. Standing beside Jayden. Glaring at me.

Marco.

Jayden stepped closer, shaking his muddy leg at me. We were just a few inches apart. His breath was warm.

In an instant, Marco was there, crammed between us. One hand was on Jayden. The other pushed me. Chills coursed through my body at his icy touch. He turned, and our eyes met. His eyes were neither light nor dark. A flat, muted gray that drew me in, pulled me toward him.

My body felt weightless. As if my feet were no longer on the ground. Light. Floating. His gaze obliterated all the gravity.

I have to get away from him, I thought. Just like Lady Azura said. Stay away. But it was so hard to focus.

Get away! my brain screamed.

With every ounce of energy I had, I wrenched my head away from him.

And then I saw the woman.

Sitting at a round table with a checked tablecloth. A stove and a microwave visible behind her.

I rubbed my eyes.

She was still there. The crease between her eyebrows deepened as she stared anxiously at a clock on the pale-green wall. Her fingers worked furiously, silently shredding a paper napkin, methodically pulling away strips. A ceramic bowl filled with red apples sat in the middle of the table.

What was happening? Where was I? This wasn't Elber's.

I leaned back and felt the slight vibrations of the refrigerator on my legs. A stainless steel sink with a few dishes stacked inside. A kitchen. I was in a kitchen.

The woman didn't seem to notice me. Her eyes left the clock only to dart to the cell phone resting alongside the pile of confettied napkin. Clock. Phone. Clock.

Her pulse quickened as her anxiety mounted.

I wrapped my arms around my ribs. My breathing was short and quick.

The second hand on the clock reached twelve, and the ticking of the next minute reverberated through my body. My eyes were drawn to the numbers. I couldn't understand why the hands moved so slowly.

The woman stopped shredding. Her nervous fingers played with the ends of her thick, shoulder-length brown hair. Her dark eyes betrayed her inner pain. Phone. Clock. Phone.

My heart thrashed in my chest. Anxiety pumped through my veins. I felt an intense fear. Her fear.

Her fear now inside me.

He's okay. He's okay. A voice repeating those words. A prayer. *Please, let him be okay.*

Thoughts. Not mine. Hers. Her thoughts in my head.

Her thoughts, bringing me back to that day. The day she waited and waited. The day the clock kept ticking. The day he didn't come home. The day the phone rang.

The hospital. A man's voice she didn't know. A man's voice filled with practiced compassion. A man who was paid to deliver bad news.

A man who said her son was not coming home.

A man who said her son had been in an accident. A terrible accident.

The tears ran down her cheeks. Her shoulders shook with a grief so deep it was unbearable. I felt her grief. It penetrated every cell in my body. He was gone. Gone forever. The woman blurred before me. Emptiness surrounded me.

Surrounded her.

Us.

And then the dread started. The terror that it could happen again.

That it would happen again.

He was late. He should have been home by now.

Our tear-filled gazes found the cell phone. We needed to call and make sure he was okay. Alive.

But he hated when the calls came. Every day. One after another.

Checking. Always checking. Making sure he was okay.

She pressed her fists to her head, trying to drive away the gnawing sense of doom. The doom that filled my head too.

Unable to bear it any longer, she cradled the phone and began to type, one finger pressing all the worry onto the screen.

WHERE ARE YOU? WHY AREN'T YOU HOME YET????

A phone buzzed.

Louder. Louder still.

I blinked. Bright fluorescent lights startled me.

"Ugh, my mom." Jayden held up his cell for me to see.

I blinked again. I was in Elber's again with Jayden. Had I ever left?

Jayden glanced at the text on the screen. "Busted. I was supposed to run in really quickly and get her bread. She gets crazy when I'm late." He typed something back quickly. Then he grabbed a random loaf of bread and hurried to the counter. He shoved some wrinkled bills at Mr. Elber.

Seconds later he was heading out the door. "See ya, Sara," he called over his shoulder. Marco followed him. I stood dazed. What had just happened?

That woman. That sad, nervous woman. I suddenly knew exactly who she was.

Jayden's mom. Marco's mom too.

I had been in Jayden's kitchen. I was sure of it. I had been watching his mom worry about him. *Feeling* his mom worry about him.

I tried to swallow, but couldn't. My mouth was painfully dry.

I didn't understand. How did I do that? Why did I do that?

I glanced down at the box of toothpaste still in my hand. It seemed so silly. So insignificant. Who cared if teeth were white? The unbearable ache of loss still filled me, made me want to run home and pull the covers over my head. And the fear. The fear of not knowing whether it was going to happen again.

Marco was trying to make sure it didn't happen again. He was protecting Jayden to protect his mother.

Suddenly I understood. Marco had touched me and showed me the pain he fought so hard to keep away from his family.

I understood. Mrs. Mendes had suffered. She still suffered.

I shuffled down the cosmetics aisle toward the spices, my thoughts fixated on Marco.

Marco wanted to protect his brother from danger.

But what did that have to do with me?

Was I dangerous?

Chapter 6

I couldn't move my arms to peel my orange.

I glanced up and down the long, skinny cafeteria table. We were wedged together so tightly. Apples were the way to go. Just lift and bite. The key was to eat food that needed minimal movement. That's probably why the sandwich was invented.

Lily pushed up against one side of me. Avery was jammed against the other. Miranda, Tamara, and Marlee sat across from us. There were tables scattered throughout with more room, but they were mostly populated by singles—kids here purely to consume food. Squishing together showed that you were part of a group. In my old school, I was a single.

"Did you get the invite?" Miranda asked the group.

"I love the silver writing on the black," Lily said. "Very Halloween but still very classy."

"I couldn't believe she sent me one," Tamara remarked. "I barely know Dina. Her mom must have made her. She's in a book club with my mom."

I studied the sparkly blue polish on my nails. I'd done them last night, but already my thumb had chipped. I hadn't gotten an invite.

"Dina takes Contemporary Jazz with us," Miranda explained. "She's been in our dance class for a couple of years, right, Lily?"

Lily rolled her eyes. "Doesn't make her any nicer to us."

"You shouldn't go," Avery piped in. "I have a gymnastics meet in Pennsylvania on Halloween weekend anyway. Dina's nasty."

"Everyone will be there," Miranda pointed out. "Lots of the cute boys. Lots of eighth graders."

"I won't be there," Avery reminded her.

"Me either," I add softly. Would Jayden? I wondered.

Lily turned. "Really? She didn't invite you?"

"Dina will never get over that the new girl in seventh grade beat her out for Harvest Queen. Ever."

Avery smiled at me, revealing the pink rubber bands
that now covered her braces.

"I don't care," I said. I didn't really. The only thing I
knew about Dina Martino was the evil eye she flashed
me in the hallway.

"We see Dina at dance this afternoon," Lily said. "I
bet she just forgot to put you on the list because you're
new. I'll ask her about it."

"You don't have to," I said.

"But we *want* you there with us." Lily tried to wrap
her arm around me, but she couldn't maneuver it, so
she settled for a bump of our shoulders.

"Definitely," Tamara chimed in.

Being part of this group is worth the citrus sacrifice, I
thought. I tossed my uneaten orange in my lunch bag
and smiled at my friends.

Island. Archipelago. I tucked my legs under me and
flipped through the pile of index cards. I had written
landforms in different shades of green marker. Bodies
of water were in blue. I always made color-coded flash
cards.

I leaned against the pillows on my teal and

raspberry comforter, trying to find a comfortable study position. There wasn't one.

"Hey, kiddo. How's it going?" Dad appeared in my bedroom doorway.

"Fine. I think I know half," I mumbled, motioning to my flash cards.

Dad frowned. "Half is fifty percent. That's failing."

"I know, I know. It's only seven o'clock. I have plenty of time to learn the rest."

"So you've got it under control?" His eyes danced as he smiled at me.

"Yes, Daddy-o. I've got it under control!"

He walked the few steps over to my bed and sat down. He seemed nervous as he thumbed through my flash cards. He cleared his throat. "So . . . I'm going out tonight," he said finally.

"Now?" I studied his outfit. Khakis, blue button-down shirt. Nothing alarming, except they'd been ironed. Or pressed by a dry cleaner. Dad was the wrinkle king. Even his work suits usually looked napped in. "Where are you going?"

"Dinner. Dinner with a friend from work."

I looked up and realized that his hair was neatly

combed, his unruly waves smoothed down with a little gel.

He was going on a date, I realized. And he was nervous about telling me.

For some reason, my dad always gets nervous about telling me when he starts dating someone new. I don't know why. I don't mind that he has girlfriends sometimes. I don't always like them, but none of them have been very long term anyway. And I just want him to be happy.

He looked at me as if he was waiting for me to say something else, but I just nodded. "Okay, have fun."

Dad put my flash cards down. "I won't be home late. Lady Azura's downstairs if you need anything. Maybe she could test you on social studies."

I raised my eyebrows. I couldn't see that happening. She regarded homework as silly. She was always saying it robbed us of a childhood of exploration. That our generation's minds were so clogged with useless facts and figures and music lyrics that we'd become closed off to the forces of nature.

Dad laughed. His blue eyes crinkled at the corners. "Okay, maybe that wasn't the best suggestion. Actually, she said something about this being facial night, but you can pop in if you want."

I doubted that. Beautifying was a sacred ritual to her.

"Love you, kiddo." Dad waved and headed down the stairs and out the front door.

I wondered who she was. I hoped she was nice. I knew he'd tell me more if things got "serious."

Dad had been dating someone in California, but they broke up before we moved here. Moving here had come out of the blue. One day he just announced that he'd gotten a new job and we were moving to a small town on the New Jersey shore. And then we left. He still hadn't given me a good reason why we came here. I didn't buy that it was his job. I was pretty sure there were lots of jobs at insurance companies in California. Or at least at insurance companies closer to home in California than New Jersey was.

I lay back on my bed and stared at the pictures on my wall. My mom's photographs. My eyes settled on the photo of the little angel figurine.

The creak of the rocking chair filled my head. The woman in the pink bedroom, rocking away her sorrow. Her sobs filled the dusty corners of the house. Her grief kept her here, I realized. I didn't know why she was sad. I knew nothing about her. Except that she was dead.

Secrets. Even the dead had them.

Not just me. Not just Dad.

Everyone.

I bolted up. If I lay here, I wouldn't study, I knew. I'd be listening. To the spirit who paced our family room. To the spirit in the sailor's hat who tapped the windowpane as he stared out across the bay. Searching. Waiting. I didn't know what for.

My bare feet hurried along the cold wooden boards and up to the third floor. I flicked on the light, bathing my craft room in a soft yellow glow. Slipping into my desk chair, I inserted my camera's memory card into the computer.

The room was back in order, or at least as much order as it ever had. The closet door was slightly ajar, but everything was quiet. It had been since that day with Lily.

I scrolled through my photos. Lady Azura cleaning her crystal ball. I liked how I'd caught her reflection in the glass and the faraway look in her eyes. I'd brought my camera to school, too, and taken a lot of pictures: Lily clowning around in front of her locker, Avery walking on her hands, and a boy I didn't know balancing under a pile of binders.

All the people in my photos were doing something, so that made them action shots. Yet they weren't *active*. There was no spark.

I had a stack of my mom's old pictures in a drawer, and I pulled them out. I chose a few from the top of the pile and spread them out before me: a field of flowers, a mailbox on a dirt road, a scattering of crumbs outside a ceramic cookie jar. I printed my four best shots onto glossy photo paper and taped them to the wall beside my mom's shots.

I stepped back for a better look and groaned. Each of Mom's photos was more alive and told more of a story than my photos of humans. I took another step back, trying to understand why. What was her secret? I wished she were still alive. I wished I could talk to her.

My photo of Lily fluttered to the ground. I scooped it up and pressed the tape harder to the yellow wall.

Then I stepped back to look again.

There's got to be a better shot I missed, I thought. I turned back to the computer and heard the slight slap of paper hitting the wood floor.

Lily's photo again.

I checked the window. The little Christmas lights were dark, and the window was closed. No breeze.

I hung the photo again with a fresh piece of tape. Then I sat in front of the screen, running through my choices. Lily's photo slipped. *Again?* I thought, annoyed. Then the photo next to it fell. And the one next to that one. The fine hairs on my arms rose as the fourth photo dropped.

I narrowed my eyes at the photos now resting on the floor. My hands clamped my thighs through my flannel pajama bottoms. Every nerve jumped to action, sensing a presence in the room.

The tape wasn't the problem. The photos hadn't dropped on their own. Someone was pulling them down.

I took a deep breath.

The spirit from the closet was back.

I twisted about, searching. Nothing.

Who was it? Before I had only been able to make out a hand. What did it look like?

I wanted to stand but couldn't will my limbs to move. Spots of light danced before me, causing my head to throb.

Then I saw him.

He was not what I'd expected.

He was so small. A young boy. Short, dark hair and dark eyes. In shorts and a cap. He reminded me of Lily's little brother.

He undulated before me. Shimmering. Pulsing in the speckled light.

He was bent over, laughing. Giggling. Slapping his skinny leg.

I stared back at him, wide-eyed. Frozen in place.

He reached for a bucket of foam craft pieces on the book shelf. With a mischievous glint in his eyes, he raised the plastic bucket and flipped it over. Pastel stars and hearts rained down, covering the floor.

He laughed, and I heard myself giggle.

As if I were elsewhere, listening to myself.

The spirit grabbed a container of red glitter. Dancing

in place, he flung the glitter into the air with unrestrained delight.

I followed the arc of crimson sparkles, and I suddenly felt a surge of uncontrollable energy. I needed to be part of this mayhem. I needed to throw things too. To make a mess with him.

I grasped a handful of paper clips and swung my arm over my head. The silver clips scattered everywhere. Laughter bubbled inside me and escaped through my mouth with volcanic force. Not my usual laugh, but the laughter of someone crazy.

The sound of my own crazy laughter made me snap out of it. Then my body convulsed, shaking with fear.

What was I doing?

Chapter 7

Out of control.

No thinking. Just moving. I had to break away.

I reached toward the spirit. The shimmery outline of the boy fell back toward the wide-open closet door. As fast as I could, I reached for the door, slamming it shut, returning him to the closet's depths. My eyes flitted about the room. Searching, searching. I dragged the small bookcase across the floor and wedged it against the door. Would that hold a ghost in? Would anything?

I didn't know. My feet pounded down the stairs. My brain felt scrambled. I had to get away.

Away from the spirit.

Away from myself.

I burst into the kitchen. The single light burning

above the sink silhouetted Lady Azura's slight frame. She turned, and I screamed.

Green slime dripped from her cheeks. Her pupils were so dilated her eyes seemed solid black in the shadows. Had the spirit done this to her?

I began to back out of the kitchen, unable to stop staring.

Her face. Oh, her horrible face!

"What's wrong, Sara?" Her lips barely moved.

"Y-you—your face—upstairs—I—" My mouth couldn't form the words.

"Oh yes." She patted her rotting cheeks with her hands. "Avocado oatmeal face mask. Quite ugly, yes, but it brings about such beauty." She turned back to the sink and simultaneously washed and scraped the gunk from her face while I concentrated on calming my breathing. In. Out. *Just part of her facial,* I told myself. *She's fine. The spirit did not do anything to her.*

I sank into one of the chairs around the kitchen table.

"Mix that yogurt with the honey, please," Lady Azura called from the sink.

I mechanically dumped the yogurt and honey into a

bowl already sitting on the table. My hand still trembled as I stirred them with a wooden spoon. "What are you cooking?"

"Do I ever cook?" Her sharp laugh was like a bark. "We're making a moisturizing facial cream. Natural hydration. Now add the ground almonds." She sat across from me as I continued to stir. Her clean face had a pinkish glow. "Who caused you to fling yourself down the stairs like that?"

"How did you know it was a *who*?" I asked tentatively.

She grinned. "My child, with us, it's always a *who*. And then we must endeavor to discover the *why*."

I told her about the spirit of the young boy in the cap.

"Ahh, Henry's at it again." She shook her head in amazement. "I forgot all about him. Imagine that."

"Who's Henry?"

"Henry is a very mischievous little boy, though I gather you've deduced that for yourself. As I recall, Henry met his end at the age of eight, back in 1920-something. It's hard for me to keep all the dates around here straight. I probably should write them down."

"You've seen Henry too?"

"Henry and I are very well acquainted. Or at least we used to be, when I could climb those steep stairs. It's been years since I've been on the second or third floors of this house. As you know, I have never even seen your room or craft room!" She reached for the bowl and began to stir. "Henry made life interesting. Always throwing things, causing havoc. Why, once he even draped himself in a bedsheet and paraded through the halls while we were having a party. I had a tricky time explaining that to my guests."

"Is he dangerous?" My mind kept returning to what he'd done to me. How he'd made me act and feel so out of control. How he'd made me not me.

"I never used to think so, but danger sniffs out young mischief makers. Years ago Henry found a box of matches lying around. He lit them. He almost burned down this house. Obviously, I had to put an end to that kind of behavior. I'm not one for unruly children."

"How did you stop him?"

"I locked him in the closet on the third floor." Lady Azura continued to stir.

"You locked a ghost in a closet?" I repeated in disbelief.

"Exactly. I told him to leave and he refused, so I locked him away. Worked so well, I forgot about him. Completely. Until he came out." She squinted at me. Her eyes seemed much smaller without her fake lashes. "He can leave anytime, you know. He chooses not to. So I choose to keep him locked away." The spoon made scraping noises against the side of the bowl. "He appeared the other day with Lily, right?"

"How'd you know?"

"Makes sense." She placed her finger into the bowl, then licked it. "Perfect. Shall I put some on your face too? Even someone as lovely as you can benefit from natural beauty remedies. You won't be young forever, you know."

"Maybe later." I leaned across the table, my elbows resting on the pale pink tablecloth. "Makes sense how?"

"Henry is a Randazzo. I don't know if you've noticed, but that family has more relatives than the TV has channels." She propped up a round magnifying mirror and, with the back of the spoon, spread the thick, ivory-colored glop on her forehead. "Lily's presence in the room must have drawn him out somehow. A family bond is very powerful. Connection through the blood."

That's why he reminded me of Lily's brother. "Why is he still here?" I asked.

"Henry is different from other spirits trapped in this realm." Lady Azura tried to speak without disturbing the concoction on her face. It reminded me of something I'd once dipped vegetables into at a party. "Henry has no agenda. He likes it here. He's just here to amuse himself."

"Well, he's not amusing me," I grumbled. I flaked the blue polish off my pinkie nail, fumbling to explain what had happened upstairs. How his emotions had become mine. As I tried, Lady Azura's eyes grew wide even under the layer of yogurt.

"Sara, you need to listen carefully. Three things. One is Henry. I don't know what he is capable of. I haven't seen him in many years, but the boy can and will certainly wreak havoc if not contained."

"Contained?"

"Keep that closet *closed*." Her voice grew louder when she said "closed."

"That will work?"

"With Henry, at his age, yes. Others, no. But now we are concerned with Henry. Understand?" I nodded. Her mood had changed dramatically. She was deadly serious.

"Second thing. You are in charge. This is your house now. That is *your* room. Not Henry's. You need to be firm. Assert yourself."

I nodded. "Firm, okay."

"Finally, this linking in with the spirits that you did, it troubles me. You can't lose yourself to them. You must set boundaries."

"Boundaries?" I kept repeating words, because I couldn't take it all in. I'd never been good at asserting myself, and now she thought I could assert myself to control dead people. How?

"Boundaries with your mind. Boundaries with your body. You must stay in control at all times. Do not allow this little boy to override you."

Should I tell her about Marco and his mom? I wondered. That I had been in his mom's head? That I felt what she felt?

"Come with me," Lady Azura ordered. She reached for a towel and wiped the yogurt mixture from her face. Bits of the goop clung to the skin by her ears, but she'd already thrown down the towel and was scurrying to her fortune-telling room. I hurried to catch up.

She stopped in front of the shelves that lined the back wall. In the dim light from the small fringed lamp, she surveyed her display of multicolored crystals. "Citrine . . . agate . . . peach moonstone." She mumbled the names under her breath as her fingertips grazed the stones.

"Hematite," she finally announced. She picked up a metallic-gray polished stone and dropped it into my palm. "This stone will deepen the connection between your soul and your body. It will help you keep your sense of self and your sense of purpose firm."

The small, smooth stone felt cool in my hand. "It's really shiny."

"Hematite's shininess will help you deflect the emotions of others," she said. "Let it remind you to enforce boundaries."

"Should I keep these?" I gestured to the ruby and aquamarine crystals dangling around my neck.

"Of course. Those are for you to keep. There's a tiny hole in the hematite as well. Add it on."

I strung the hematite alongside the aquamarine and ruby crystal. The metallic gray stone radiated power next to the clear red and pale turquoise. Would it work? Would it keep the spirits out of my head? Did I even want it to work?

For Henry, yes. But I was intrigued by Jayden's mom and his life, even though experiencing her grief and worry disturbed me. I got to peer through a secret window into his world. Now I wanted to know more. I wanted to know what Jayden thought and why Marco guarded him. Was that wrong?

I was afraid Lady Azura would say it was. She'd insist I set the boundaries she kept talking about. But did I really need to? Henry and Jayden's brother, although both dead, were very different.

At least, I thought they were.

Chapter 8

Happy day, happy day, happy day, I sang to myself as Miss Klingert read aloud the lab partners. I was paired with Jayden. I pressed the ruby crystal with my thumb and forefinger. *Keep working,* I encouraged it.

I met Jayden at our assigned lab table, where Christine Wu and A.J. Carpenter waited for us. We often did labs with them. Marco waited too. He stood silently to the side, his expression blank. I decided to ignore him.

I watched A.J. wrinkle his forehead, deep in concentration. He methodically placed one sugar cube on top of another, building a tower. We were supposed to use the cubes to test the effects of various chemicals on erosion. Jayden joined in.

Christine glanced toward the teacher, who was

helping another group set up their experiments. "She's not going to like that," she warned.

"Almost done," A.J. murmured. He straightened a cube. The tower was already a foot high.

"Steady, man," Jayden cautioned as the sugar skyscraper swayed.

"We need to start the lab," Christine reminded them.

"Yeah, yeah." Jayden waved her off. There was one white cube left. Jayden slid it across the table to me. "Let's see what you've got."

I felt him watching me as I studied the angle of the tower. I slowly rested the cube on top. The tower trembled. We all held our breath.

"Sweet!" Jayden said. I knew he was talking about the tower, but I pretended that he was talking about me. I couldn't help grinning, as he took a deep breath and blew the tower down.

"Are you going in costume to Dina's?" Christine asked Jayden as we lined up our lab supplies.

"It's a costume party?" he asked.

"I thought so. But maybe not." She turned to me. "Do you know?"

I didn't, of course, because I wasn't invited. A minute earlier I would have told her that and not cared, but now I did care. Jayden was going to the party. Everyone was going to the party. Everyone except me.

"Nope," I said. My gaze settled on the translucent form of Marco. Marco had a strange, satisfied-looking smirk on his face. Was he glad I wasn't invited? Then I had a horrifying thought. Had he somehow manipulated the invites, so I wouldn't be at a party with Jayden? I narrowed my eyes at him. Could a spirit do that?

"Someone will know." Christine twisted on her stool. "I'll ask Marlee when we're done."

"Whatever," said Jayden. He placed a sugar cube in a petri dish. He didn't seem to care about Dina's party. He probably went to a different party every weekend, I figured.

"Well, it's not like you'll show up anyway," Christine said.

"I might," Jayden replied.

"Oh, please. You never go anywhere. You decline every invite! You always have an excuse," Christine countered.

Jayden waved his hand like he didn't care. "What can I say? I'm a busy guy." But I knew he was lying. I watched his shoulders tense and his posture stiffen. Christine had gotten to him.

Suddenly it made sense to me. Jayden might be invited to all the parties, but he never went. He didn't want to worry his mom. Or maybe his mom wouldn't let him leave the house. Either way, I knew this to be true the same way a mother lion can sense when her cub is in danger. I knew it deep inside me, as if I were the one worried for his safety.

"Time to get busier," I said, handing him a beaker of yellow liquid to change the subject. "Let's do this." My hand brushed his, and he caught my eye. I smiled.

Jayden's secret.

I gazed back at Marco, who was clearly fuming at our slight touch.

Secrets, plural, I thought. There were many secrets to keep.

I handed Lady Azura the brown bag filled with her honey, yogurt, and Swedish fish from my afternoon Elber's run as the doorbell rang.

"Maybe another new client," Lady Azura said hopefully. "Go see."

I flung open the front door. "Oh, it's you."

Lily stood on our porch. I couldn't hide my disappointment for Lady Azura. Our flyers and posting had gotten her a bit of business, but people were far from lining up on our sidewalk. Very far.

"Nice. Real nice greeting." Lily wore a black leotard and black stretch dance pants. She moved to step into the house, but I blocked her path. She shifted to the left. I moved with her, blocking her again. "What's with you? Can't I come in?"

She couldn't. I had vowed she'd never enter again. Henry had remained locked in the third-floor closet for the past few days. At least I thought he had. I was avoiding the third floor, but I didn't want her Randazzo-ness drawing him out.

"Well, I'm kind of busy." I tried to answer without answering. I couldn't tell her I had to keep the living people away from the dead people.

"With what?" Lily demanded, her hands resting on her hips.

"Let the poor girl in the house." Lady Azura grabbed

Lily's hand with her free hand. "The manners of your generation are abysmal. My mother would never abide leaving a guest waiting on the porch."

I stared as Lily waltzed past me into the house. This was the beginning of trouble, I knew. Big trouble.

"Now, to what do we owe the pleasure?" Lady Azura asked as if she were greeting a guest at the queen's palace. Lady Azura wore a long, silky olive-green skirt with a matching flowy top. She'd knotted a tan-and-navy scarf around her waist. She always dressed as if she were expecting company, but few people ever came over. Lily had provided the perfect opportunity to entertain.

"I just came from dance. I wanted to tell Sara something. And talk to you, too," Lily said. She wasn't just being polite. Lily seriously enjoyed hanging out with Lady Azura. The two of them could debate the merits of mauve lip gloss for hours. With them, the huge gap between their ages didn't matter.

"Excellent. Let's visit." Lady Azura led Lily through the foyer and into the kitchen at the back. "Snacks. I shall prepare snacks." I trailed behind. Lady Azura rested the paper bag on the counter and opened the refrigerator.

"I talked to Dina." Lily tried to sound casual, but her tone betrayed her. I knew she hadn't gotten an invitation for me.

"Did she forget about me or does she not like me?" I asked.

"Hates you is more like it."

Lady Azura popped her head out of the fridge. "How could anyone hate our Sara?"

"Sara beat out Dina to be Harvest Queen. Dina has believed she was queen of the universe since she was old enough to strut down a hallway, but then Sara came along and won. It bummed her out big-time." She turned to me. "Not inviting you to her Mischief Night party is a revenge thing."

I didn't even know Dina, but the thought of her not liking me made my stomach queasy. I suspected she'd turned her popular eighth-grade girlfriends against me, even though most probably didn't know who I was. Would she try to convert the kids in my grade too?

I gave an exaggerated shrug, like it didn't matter.

"Parties aren't my thing." Especially now, I thought, since Jayden wouldn't be showing up.

I thought ahead to the night before Halloween. Apparently they called it Mischief Night in Stellamar. We didn't have a name for it in California, but it was the same night. The night kids toilet-papered trees and ding-dong-ditched houses. It was also the night spirits moved about. Not like I saw them now. That night they were everywhere. Agitated. Active. Wandering. Scary. Even in California, where the spirits had mostly left me alone, it was a night I dreaded all year. I couldn't even imagine what it was going to be like in Stellamar, where spirits lived in my house and approached me on a regular basis. Mischief Night was actually the perfect name for this dreaded night. It was a night I always stayed home, wrapped in a comforter, watching cartoons. No scary movies for me. Real life was scary enough. I planned on doing the same this year.

"If this Dina girl is so mean, though I suspect her meanness is really a disguise for her insecurity, why would Lily want to go to her party?" Lady Azura asked me, although it was obvious the question was really directed at Lily.

"Lots of kids will be there," I offered. "Everyone at school is talking about it."

"I'm not going," Lily announced, anger now spiking her voice. "Dina thinks she's so great, but she's not. She can't dump on my friend and then think I'm showing up for her party."

"Thanks, Lil, but you don't have to—"

"Yes, she does," Lady Azura cut in. She plopped the bag of red Swedish fish, a bowl of raspberries, and a pitcher of pink lemonade on the table. She liked to color-coordinate food. "Lily understands that the power of friendship should dominate the power plays of silly girls. Besides, Lily has other plans that night."

"I do?"

"She does?" I echoed.

"Lily has been invited to my party. My legendary party."

"Really?" Lily bounced with excitement. "My mom only went once, but she still talks about it. I thought just adults were invited, though. I thought you chose a small group of people whose karma was connected in some way."

"I used to, but this year will be different. Change is

in the air." She turned to me and smiled. "This year, I have just decided I will be having a Blue Moon party on October thirtieth, and I will invite people of all ages, including you girls and your friends. We'll make it an open house."

"A Blue Moon party?" I asked.

"Precisely." Lady Azura noticed our blank stares. "You girls don't know about a blue moon?" She nibbled a Swedish fish. "Usually we have one full moon a month, or twelve a year. But about every three years, there is an extra full moon—a thirteenth full moon. That rare thirteenth full moon is called the blue moon."

"What happens when there's a blue moon?" I hoped my eyes conveyed what I was really trying to ask. If Mischief Night riled up the spirits, would a blue moon on Mischief Night make it worse?

"Anything can happen on a blue moon." Her eyes twinkled. "It's a magical night."

"Yes, anything!" Lily jumped in. "This party will have mystical and spooky all rolled together. I can't wait to tell everyone."

All the kids from my school, here, at my house on the night the spirits were at their most active? My heart thumped an irregular beat just imagining it.

"What about Dina?" I asked. "She did send out invites first. It wouldn't be right to have a party at the same time." I wasn't really concerned about Dina's feelings or social manners, but I was scrambling to come up with a way to stop this party. I *had* to stop it.

"What about Dina?" Lily raised her eyebrows. "She can still have her party. Now kids have a choice. Choice is a good thing."

"That it is," Lady Azura agreed, sharing a partners-in-party-planning grin with Lily. "My late-night days have long passed, so my party will start early. Your friends can come here first, and if they are inclined to leave, they can proceed on to that girl's fete."

"Or not," Lily finished. "If you do fortune-telling, everyone in town will come. And you'll get new business."

"Now that's an idea. This party will have to be planned." She gathered the small notepad by the phone, and a pen. "What we need is a list."

"We should decorate using a midnight-blue theme. You know, to combine blue moon with Halloween spooky. I think it's much more fashion-forward than the orange-and-black thing," Lily suggested. She and

Lady Azura scooted chairs next to each other and bent their heads over the list. Decorations, food, and the rearranging of furniture were discussed and analyzed.

I ate all the raspberries. One after the other. I couldn't think of anything else to do. I'd temporarily lost my new best friend to the charms of an elderly party planner.

"Oh, goodness, look at the clock," Lady Azura said suddenly. "The dry cleaner closes at five, and I desperately need my lavender skirt. You'll go, Sara?"

I nodded. The more I listened to their menu suggestions, the more my growing sense of panic made breathing something I had to think about. I couldn't imagine why she urgently needed the skirt, but I didn't feel like asking. I just wanted to leave—and take Lily with me.

"Come on, Lil," I said. "We can grab your bike on the way."

"I'm going to hang here for a while, if that's okay, and come up with fake scares. You know, cold spaghetti for brains, a fog machine for ghosts, maybe a dangling skeleton. What else can we do?"

"Record spooky noises to play throughout the

night," Lady Azura suggested. "Screams and groans and footsteps and—"

"What about crying and the creak of a rocking chair?" I finished. I knew my tone was a bit nasty, but I couldn't help it. I was angry with Lady Azura. What was she doing? Having a party on Mischief Night out of pity for me wasn't going to be fun. It was going to be a disaster. She should have asked me first. She knew spirits wandered about, and she especially knew about Henry. Didn't she understand how high the potential for disaster and ultimate humiliation was for me?

I turned to go.

"Sara, wait—" Lady Azura started.

I wasn't going to stay and help plan a party that was sure to end with everyone making fun of my obviously haunted house. "They're going to close. Be back soon," I called over my shoulder.

I needed to get far away. For now, the dry cleaner would have to do.

I'd calmed down by the time I pedaled home. I concentrated on the *thwamp, thwamp* the plastic bag covering the skirt made as it flapped in the breeze. I still wasn't happy about the party. But I had a plan to talk to Lady Azura quietly. Calmly. Rationally. Get her to cancel it. I practiced my speech in my head. I hoped Lily was already gone.

A blue dirt bike rested against the bottom porch step. I groaned. My speech would have to wait. One of Lily's brothers must be here too. Was it Sam or Joey? I didn't recognize the bike.

The familiar scent of cinnamon greeted me as I let myself in the front door. Cinnamon candles burning meant clients. The heavy purple curtains were drawn across Lady Azura's rooms. The low rumble of voices drifted into the foyer.

I hadn't been gone long. I wondered who'd shown up.

I kicked off my sneakers and padded quietly down the hallway.

"Sara! Sara!" Lily repeated my name in an urgent whisper. She stood steps away from the purple curtain.

"What?"

"Shh!" Lily grabbed my arm and pulled me close. "Oh my God, oh my God, oh my God! You are never going to believe it. Never!" She shifted her weight from foot to foot, unable to hold back her news. "Guess who came to see Lady Azura with one our flyers—*our flyers*—and wanted to get a reading!"

"Who?" I whispered.

"Totally blew my mind when the doorbell rang. We thought it was you. Lady Azura answered. I was in the kitchen, but I saw him. He didn't see me, but *I saw him!*" Lily's whispered words ran into one another as her excitement grew. "You have to see this."

She grabbed my hand and pulled me toward the curtain before I could protest. Slowly she peeled back a corner of the heavy velvet.

My eyes took a moment to adjust to the dimness. The only light was the reddish glow cast on the walls by the candles. Lady Azura sat in her big armchair. Her client was across from her, his back to us.

Thick brown wavy hair.

My mouth opened wide. Wider. Until I couldn't open it any more.

Jayden. Jayden was getting his fortune told by Lady Azura!

Chapter 9

Jayden sat across from Lady Azura, talking about . . . talking about . . .

I tried to rewind my thoughts. What had I told Lady Azura? Had I told her I liked Jayden? Had I ever called him by name? Did she know who he was?

He'd come because of me, I realized. *I made that flyer.*

Lady Azura poured boiling water from her enamel teakettle into a porcelain cup. She was about to read his tea leaves.

I stepped back into the hallway. Lily followed.

"I knew I'd have to scrape you off the ceiling." Lily beamed. "Amazing, right? Aren't you dying to know why he's here?"

"What do you think Lady Azura is telling him?"

"That you are supposed to be his girlfriend. That he was meant to fall in love with you."

My forehead grew warm. Could Lady Azura really be saying such things?

"Let's spy," Lily urged, heading toward the curtain.

"No way," I whispered. "He came to talk to her about a private thing."

"What if that private thing is you?' Lily asked. "What if he's not really here to see her? What if the fortune-telling thing is a cover? Maybe he's just pretending so he has an excuse to visit you!"

My cheeks were now the same pinkish color as my forehead. Could Lily be right? "He doesn't know I live upstairs." At least, I didn't think he did.

"I'm seeing what's going on," Lily whispered. She poked her head back through the side of the curtain.

I hesitated. I knew I shouldn't, but the desire to hear what she was saying to him was too strong. *Just for a minute,* I told myself. *I'll only listen for a minute.* I slipped in next to Lily. I knew that from where we stood Jayden couldn't see us. I'd peeked in on another of Lady Azura's clients when we first moved in.

". . . but that will not occur for another year. Now

the final image that's coming to me"—Lady Azura peered at the tea leaves remaining in the white cup—"is a guitar."

"Guitar?" Jayden's voice was unmistakable. "I don't play that."

"The tea shows us symbols." Lady Azura leaned away from the cup. "The guitar sings of romance to come."

Romance. I instinctively wrapped my hand around the crystals on my necklace. *Work, work,* I chanted silently to the ruby crystal. Lily pinched my arm. I turned, and she flashed me a thumbs-up.

"And that is it," Lady Azura announced. I wondered what she'd seen in his cup before I peeked in. Did it have to do with me?

Jayden shifted in his seat but made no move to leave.

"Do you require additional services?" Lady Azura asked. She wasn't pushy. She sounded merely curious.

"I don't have any more money," Jayden said, his voice so low I had to lean forward on my toes.

"Tell me what you are searching for, and then we will discuss finances," Lady Azura said. Her face was open and welcoming.

"I didn't come here for the tea-leaf thing exactly," Jayden admitted. "I mean, it was great and all—"

"You seek answers," Lady Azura said. "For what?"

"My brother died." He rushed the words out as if he couldn't say them fast enough. "I mean, he died a long time ago, only it doesn't seem like a long time ago. You know? It's like he's more here with us dead than he ever was alive. He's all my mom ever talks about. My mom lives like something bad is going to happen again. To me. To my dad. My dad doesn't talk about Marco at all, but sometimes his not talking is worse, because either way Marco is here. My entire family revolves around his death. That's weird, right?"

"Not at all. Death is often all-encompassing. What is happening to your family is not so strange." Lady Azura waited patiently. Jayden fidgeted, seemingly unsure how or whether to proceed.

"So, um, I heard . . . I heard that you can contact the dead." Jayden stared at his hands, unable to meet Lady Azura's eyes. "Could you contact my brother?"

Lily pinched me so hard, I almost screamed. I turned to push her hand away.

Oh . . . my . . . God! she mouthed to me.

I realized that Lily didn't know about Marco. No one knew about Marco.

Marco. I scanned the darkened room. The faint outline of Marco's shimmery figure stood in the corner, arms crossed. He was not pleased.

Dread flooded my veins. I was watching a train wreck about to happen. It was as if I were on a far-off mountain peak with a clear view of the tracks, yet powerless to stop the speeding disaster.

Did Lady Azura know that the spirit Jayden wanted her to summon was already here? Did she feel his anger growing?

"Calling up the departed should be done with great forethought," Lady Azura cautioned. "Why do you want to communicate with your brother?"

"I don't know." Jayden's voice was strained. He sounded so different from how he usually sounded at school. He sounded sad and confused. Not at all confident and joking like he usually did. "It's like . . . the weight of his memory is too much. I just want him to send some sort of sign to my mom that everything will be okay. That she can stop worrying so much. . . ." His voice trailed off.

"Jayden, you still have the gift of life. You don't need your brother's blessing to live it," Lady Azura counseled.

Marco moved toward the table. His anger throbbed around him. A negative force.

Jayden stood. "This wasn't a good idea—"

"No, no." Lady Azura gripped the table, suddenly sensing Marco's presence. Unable to see him, but feeling him. His energy. His anger. "Not at all. You have a great emotional burden. You must find a way to crawl out from under this burden and assert your independence. You need to sever the cord that binds you. Release yourself from your brother."

Marco pushed himself between his brother and Lady Azura, desperate to stop the exchange. He did not want Lady Azura to counsel Jayden. His opaque eyes darted wildly around the room, as if he was looking for something to help him end the session. Then his gaze rested on me. *He saw me!*

Chills racked my body. I stared back. I couldn't look away. His eyes drew me in. Closer. Closer.

The chills gave way to comforting warmth blanketing my shoulders, as if the sun had come inside.

I blinked, opening my eyes to a brilliant blue sky. The slightest breeze with the aroma of pine tingled my nose. I wrapped my hands around my bare arms. Bare arms? I glanced down to a pink halter top and cut-off jean shorts. My legs and arms soaked up the rays of the summer sun. I sat on a striped towel.

Laughter.

I turned. Two girls and three boys sat on towels too. Older than I was. High school, probably. They laughed and shared sandwiches. The girls wore bikini tops and shorts. The boys had on bathing suits.

A bag of potato chips passed from hand to hand. The laughter of friends. Joking. Fun times. The chips passed to me. I was part of this group. This group of friendly faces I didn't know.

But I did know a face. One of the boys. Ray-Bans shaded his eyes, but the hoodie was unmistakable. His skin glowed. Caramel-colored. Alive. Vibrant. Marco.

In life, Marco bore a strong resemblance to Jayden. That same grin. Those same coffee-colored eyes.

Marco wrapped his arm playfully around a pretty girl with long blond hair. She giggled and pushed him away. He told a joke. Everyone laughed.

I heard the rush of water and glanced down. Gray-blue waters of a river swirled below me. White foam gathered around small jagged rocks. We were up high on a flat overhang. Pine trees surrounded us. Birds sang above us. The water glittered under the rays of the sun.

A perfect day.

My attention returned to Marco, as if guided by an unseen force. He pulled a chunky black cell phone from his pocket and flipped it open. Not a current model. An old phone. Ringing.

"Yes, Mom, I'm studying," he said into the receiver. He pulled the straw from his soda can and gently poked the blond girl as he talked. She giggled and elbowed him. Flirting.

"Yep, I'm at the library. Crowded today," he said, leaning closer to the girl. He obviously liked her.

The girl giggled at his lie to his mother.

"Oh, come on, Mom." Marco's playful tone changed to annoyance. "Today? I don't want—"

The girl walked her fingers up his arm.

"Yeah, yeah, I heard you." Marco snapped the phone shut. "I've got to go," he told the group. "Got to babysit my brother."

"That stinks," muttered one of the other boys.

"You can't go," the flirting girl said, feigning a pout. She walked her fingers farther up his arm. "Stay. For me."

Marco hesitated. He wanted to stay, that was clear. I could feel his indecision. That pull between family and friends. "I don't know—"

"Yes, you do." She flashed him a smile. A smile that she knew would win out.

Someone tugged my arm. I wanted to hear what Marco would say. I ignored it and instinctively reached for the crystals around my neck. I traced the contours of the stones as I watched Marco. As he looked to the smiling girl. As he made a choice.

I circled my fingers over the smooth, glassy hematite. The stone was warmer than the sun on my skin.

A tug again. I turned, and the shivers returned.

Lily.

Lily tugged at my arm. Bringing me back. Back to the folds of the velvet curtain.

She pointed, and I followed her finger. Jayden! Jayden was leaving Lady Azura's fortune-telling room. He was steps away from discovering us.

Chapter 10

Lily scurried down the hall. My socks skidded on the wooden floors as I slid behind her into the safety of the kitchen.

She bent to catch her breath. "Wow, that was close!" she whispered. "Why didn't you move? Were you in a love trance watching him?"

A love trance? No. But a different kind of trance. Marco had done something to me. He'd brought me in. Showed me another piece of their family puzzle. But why? What was happening by that river when Marco was still alive?

I heard the front door close, then the rhythmic clatter of Lady Azura's low heels. He was gone. *They* were gone.

I leaned against the back of a chair. I felt

light-headed. "Don't tell her," I warned Lily. "You can't let her know we were there."

I'd missed what had happened at the end. I guessed that Lady Azura hadn't agreed to call up Marco. I knew it wasn't because of the money. But did she promise to do it another time?

"I see you girls are still here." Lady Azura poured herself a glass of the now-warm pink lemonade. She drank, not looking at us but deep in her own thoughts.

"What did he want?" Lily asked. I prayed Lady Azura couldn't hear how fake Lily sounded.

"That I cannot tell you." She looked weary.

"Come on," Lily wheedled. "He goes to our school. Sara likes him, you know."

Lady Azura eyed me curiously, then turned to Lily. "A lawyer never tells his clients' secrets. A doctor never reveals her patients' medical issues. Likewise, I never betray my clients' trust." She made the motion of zipping her lips. "I need to lie down. That reading left me a bit drained. Sara, will you be okay?"

"Okay?" I asked. Was she talking about what had happened with Marco?

"Your dad is working late again," she reminded me.

"Oh yes. I'm fine." I was happy to be left alone. I had a lot to think about.

It was all a blur at first. Blue and gold. The green of the field. Legs pumping.

I steadied my camera and observed the action in my viewfinder. Then I trained my lens on Jayden.

His wiry frame dodged in front of the ball. I snapped, capturing the moment. Cranking up the telephoto lens, I zeroed in. Determination radiated from his eyes as he touched his foot on the ball and began to dribble up the field. With each step, I snapped a photo, hoping the results would please Mrs. Notkin. She'd asked me today when I would be submitting my photos. I promised to hand them in the Monday after Halloween, just a few days away.

Jayden faked to the left, maneuvering the ball away from the other team's burly defender. Then he passed the ball to Garrett. But I kept my lens focused on Jayden. *There are other players on the team,* the voice inside my head reminded me. *Good action shots are with the kid who has the ball.* Yet I couldn't stop watching Jayden, and the confident way he dodged every opposing player.

I bit my lip. Marco was on the field. Beside his brother, of course. But not watching. Helping.

I pressed my eye against the viewfinder, the camera pushing uncomfortably on my face. What was he doing? As each defender stepped to block or move in front of Jayden, Marco's unseen hand guided them in a different direction.

Garrett passed the ball back to Jayden. A defender moved to steal it, but Marco was there first. His shimmery foot nudged the defender's foot, forcing him to kick the air instead of the ball. Jayden pushed on, unaware of his supernatural assistance.

He slammed the ball toward the goal. It was a strong kick, but the goalie managed to catch it. Marco was a few steps too far away to help.

"The coach says Jayden has eyes in the back of his head. That's why he can move across the field like that," Lily commented. She stood next to me on the sidelines, scribbling in a notebook.

"He definitely has a second pair of eyes," I murmured, as the referee gave two shrill toots of his whistle to end the game.

"This sport is so boring," Lily complained. "Zero to

zero. How does Mrs. Notkin think I'm going to write an exciting story if nothing happens? I need a quote from the coach." She stomped across the field.

I sat on the grass as parents and kids streamed past on the way to the parking lot. I clicked through the photos I'd taken. Some had potential.

"Hey, Harvest Queen."

He stood next to me. Mud and grass caked his legs. The shoelaces of his black cleats were untied.

"Hey," I said. I remembered how upset and lonely he'd seemed in Lady Azura's room. *He needs a friend,* I thought. "Here to sell me more of your famous mud?" I joked. *I can be that friend,* I thought.

"You buying?" He squatted down beside me.

"I only buy winning mud," I remarked.

"Ouch. Not fair. We didn't lose."

"Tying isn't winning."

"Are you calling me a loser?" He pretended to be offended, but his eyes were smiling.

"No, just your lame mud. Now a signed jersey might be worth something. . . ." I tugged the hem of his and smiled. "Why is yours a different shade of blue from the others?"

"You noticed?" He seemed surprised. The difference was subtle. "Mine is vintage. Been in the family."

I bit my lip again and thought about what this meant. Then I took a risk. "Was that your brother's? The one you told me about at the dance?" During the dance last month, I'd found Jayden in the graveyard in back of the school. Marco wasn't buried there, but it had been the anniversary of his death. That was all he'd told me.

Jayden nodded. "Yeah. Marco was amazing at soccer."

"You're really good too."

Jayden didn't answer, but he stayed next to me. *Maybe he wants to talk about it,* I thought.

About Marco.

Marco, who I suddenly felt, as he hovered beside Jayden. Marco, who pulled all the air out of a bright, sunny day, making it hard for me to breathe.

I took a deep breath. "So what happened to Marco? I mean, how did he die?"

"Swimming accident." Jayden plucked blades of the grass.

Marco edged closer.

"What happened?" I asked.

Marco wrapped a protective arm around Jayden,

an arm he couldn't see but could feel, because all at once his mood changed. I could see it in his eyes. They were now guarded.

"Does it really matter?" Jayden stopped pulling up the grass. "My brother was so brave. Accidents happen to brave people too."

"They do," I said quietly. My lungs felt tight. Breathing was an effort. "He sounds great."

"Marco was the best big brother," Jayden continued. "He took care of me. He was amazing at sports, and everyone just loved him. I'm going to be just like him."

Marco's expression changed. Fear? Panic? Distress? I couldn't read his blank eyes. But something was wrong. He began to push at me. Not with his arms or his body, but with the weight of his spirit. My head throbbed. A pounding began behind my eyes, a pain that made it hard to speak to Jayden.

"I brought you players to photograph!" Lily called.

Sunlight pulsed before my eyes as I raised my head to the field. Lily headed toward us with Garrett, Luke, Jack L., and Jack R. in tow.

Marco released his grip, and immediately my

headache lessened. The autumn air turned crisp and breathable.

"Lily said you needed action shots," Luke called to me. "Watch this." He juggled the soccer ball with his knees.

"Sara." Lily now stood nearby. "The camera? You kind of need to use it."

I stared down at the camera resting in my lap, then at Marco. He remained seated, arm around Jayden. Expressionless. I tried to focus on the boys, who were now having some sort of juggling contest. "Thanks." I raised my camera and took photos, barely paying attention to my subjects.

Lily told the boys about the party at Lady Azura's house. She told them about the night of fortune-telling and food and the house filled with scares.

I watched Jayden stiffen at Lady Azura's name, but Lily was careful. She never said anything about seeing him there.

"Come on," Luke scoffed. "That house isn't really haunted, even if that fortune-teller does live there."

"Yes, it is," Lily insisted. "Ask Sara. She lives there too."

"You live with the fortune-teller?" Luke pushed his sweaty blond hair from his eyes to look at me.

"You live with her?" Jayden's voice was soft. Incredulous.

I didn't know what to say. I couldn't lie. "My dad and I live upstairs. We kind of share the house with her."

I watched as the expression on Jayden's face turned from confusion to hurt. I met his gaze and in that instant, I knew that he knew. He sprang up from the grass and stalked toward the field. Marco followed.

"Hey, where are you going?" Garrett yelled.

"Later," Jayden called without looking back.

I ran after him, panting when I reached his side.

Jayden refused to slow down. "You knew I went there yesterday?"

I wanted to be his friend. Friends tell the truth. I nodded.

"And you don't say anything? What's up with that?" he demanded.

"I'm sorry. That was wrong," I admitted, jogging to keep up. "I didn't think it was my place—"

"Today you bring up my brother, and I'm supposed

to believe that just came out of nowhere? What did she tell you?"

"Nothing. Honestly, nothing. She doesn't talk about people who come and see her," I insisted. "I just kind of figured—"

He stopped abruptly. "Did you tell all your friends I went to see some crazy fortune-teller?"

"No. I would never do that." I hoped he believed me. "And she's not crazy!"

"She was totally lame. I went as a joke, you know." He turned away and pretended to watch the younger kids practicing on the field.

I didn't believe that, but I didn't want to argue. "Lady Azura's really good. She helps a lot of people. You should come back."

"I don't need help!" he yelled. I'd never heard him yell before.

Marco was glaring at me. I sighed. *Just drop it and walk away,* I told myself. Then I heard Lily talking with the boys in the distance. Lily always tackled problems head-on, and people liked her for it. I couldn't give up on him just because he yelled.

"She has a connection with the dead," I said quietly,

ignoring Marco and moving closer to Jayden. "Come home with me now. I'm sure she'll—"

"I'm not going to your house now—"

"So come to the party this weekend. She'll be there then," I suggested.

"I'm not coming to your party!" Jayden cried, stepping away. "I'm never going to that woman again, and I'm certainly not going back to your freaky house!"

The sting would have been the same if he'd slapped me in the face. *Freaky.* My house was freaky. Next it would be me.

This is not about you, I reminded myself. Jayden needed help. He had to know that Marco's spirit was still here. He had to have it explained to him.

"Jayden, listen." I grabbed his arm, pulling him toward me. "Sometimes the dead linger. In different ways, I mean." I wished I'd had time to plan out how to say this.

From across the field, a soccer ball arced through the sky.

"Sometimes their spirit stays and your—" Before I could blurt it all out, the ball nailed me in the head, knocking me to the ground.

Chapter 11

I looked up at the stars.

Forty glow-in-the-dark stars now hung from dental floss from the ceiling of the front sitting room. I'd never seen Lady Azura use this room, but she was intent on decorating it for the party.

"Place that last one to the left of the fireplace," she instructed me.

I did what she wanted. Since I'd gotten home from the soccer field, I'd been on decorating duty. I tucked the roll of tape under my arm and rubbed my scalp with my free hand. I had a small bump, but it didn't hurt. I probably fell from the shock of being hit.

Everyone had rushed around me—Lily, all the boys, the two coaches from the field. Everyone but Marco. He stood off to the side, gloating. The ball had to have come from him. I saw those little kids practicing. No way any of them could've possibly kicked a ball that hard without a little help.

Had he sent the soccer ball my way because I touched his brother? Or had he gotten scared that I would find the words to tell Jayden about him?

"You were watching." Lady Azura handed me a shiny silver-and-black garland.

Watching what? I almost said, but didn't. I knew what she meant. I taped the garland around the doorway and said nothing.

"You and Lily." She shook her head. "I expected more from you."

"I'm sorry." Lady Azura never raised her voice, but her quiet disappointment was much more powerful. "We were wrong. It's just that Jayden was the boy I was telling you about. The boy with the spirit following him."

"And?"

"And what?"

"Just because you can see a spirit beside the boy does not give you the right to spy on him. Or me."

"I'm sorry," I said again. "But you saw how upset

having Marco, that's his brother, around makes Jayden. He upsets me, too. I just want to send him on his way, or whatever it's called. Make him not trapped here." I paused, but Lady Azura didn't reply. "I think you know how to do that. Can't you show me or tell me or something?"

She stopped arranging the garland. "You are starting in the middle of the story. We are powerless to help unless we know what has happened since page one. I do not know Jayden and Marco's story. Neither do you. Until Jayden or Marco tells one of us, there is nothing to do but set boundaries between you and the spirit."

"That's not fair. I have these abilities that other people don't have. I should be able to use them to help Jayden."

"Help Jayden?" Lady Azura gently placed her hand on my shoulder. "Be honest, Sara. Is it Jayden who you truly want to help? Or is it Sara?"

"I don't know what you're talking about."

"I think you do. You like this boy. I didn't need to hear it from Lily to know that. Marco, for whatever reason, stands between you and him. Now if Marco were no longer there, that would possibly improve things for you. Am I right?"

"No, that's not it." I crossed my arms over my chest. "It's better for Jayden and for Marco if Marco goes."

"And you know this how? Because you are alive? Does being alive make you smarter?" she challenged.

I didn't know the answer to that.

"The only way a guardian spirit will depart is if he is expelled by the person he guards," she explained in a measured voice. "Jayden is the only one who can show Marco to the door. Not you. Jayden has to want him gone and express it."

"But how can Jayden tell someone to leave if he doesn't even know he's there?" This was all so frustrating.

"Jayden is on the journey now. It's a long road to understanding and acceptance of what he cannot see but can only feel."

"Then you need to help him," I implored. "If I get him to come back, will you help? You heard him say his brother is a weight on his family. Jayden's life would be so much better without Marco getting in the way."

"And I suspect, my dear, Marco would say the same about you." Lady Azura pressed her crimson lips together, holding back a grin. She picked up another garland and set about hanging it as I silently fumed.

"This looks spooktacular!" Dad called as he opened the front door. We'd decorated the foyer as well.

I ran out to greet him. Seeing him always made me happy. When I was little, we called ourselves the Two Musketeers. We'd do everything together. We even bought matching shirts for the weekends. Weekend shirts meant fun times together.

As I hugged him, I smelled an unfamiliar scent on his blue button-down shirt. Something perfumey. I pulled back. "You have a girlfriend," I said.

"Sort of." He blushed the same pink as I always did. "How'd you know?"

"You smell like lilac." In the past, he'd smelled like roses, berries, and vanilla. A new scent meant a new girlfriend.

Dad sniffed. "I thought I smelled like coffee."

"Lilac's nice." I tried to be supportive.

"You'll like her. Janelle works at the insurance company too. She's really smart, and a lot of fun." He smiled awkwardly and then put his arm around my shoulder, drawing me close.

"Will you stay home for dinner tonight?" I asked.

I didn't want to ask too many questions about Janelle. Not yet.

"Definitely. I'll make my famous chili." Dad dropped his briefcase on the floor by the narrow hall table. "Majorly spicy or extra spicy?"

"Extra-extra." We both liked our food spicy.

"I'll tone a batch down for you," he promised Lady Azura, who now held an oversize leather handbag. "Are you ready to go?"

"Indeed." Today was beauty salon day. Dad always made sure he was home in time to drive her.

"Homework done and then we'll cook," Dad instructed as he left with Lady Azura.

I thought about my book bag waiting in the kitchen with all the worksheets. Then I spotted my camera resting on the table where I'd left it after the soccer smackdown. Had I gotten any good photos?

I scrolled through the memory card. The boys juggling in a circle was an excellent shot. Jayden dribbling the ball downfield. Jayden pulling his leg back to kick. Yes, these were good enough to submit. I would print them out and turn them in to Mrs. Notkin.

Looking at the pictures, I couldn't help but think

about Jayden. He had walked away from the field after seeing that I was okay. No good-bye. No apology for yelling. He was still angry with me. I hated that.

I pulled out my phone and texted him. **I'M SORRY. REALLY.**

Then I waited.

He didn't answer.

PLEASE COME TO THE PARTY.

Again no reply.

I knew his mom wasn't big on parties. I tried once more. **BRING YOUR PARENTS 2 PARTY 2. IT'S AN OPEN HOUSE THING.**

I wasn't expecting an answer. He was mad. I got it.

I fiddled with my necklace. Courage. Boundaries. Love. None of the crystals were working.

I pushed back the velvet curtains and entered Lady Azura's darkened fortune-telling room. Weak late-afternoon sun filtered through the front window. I stood before the shelves arrayed with crystals and gemstones. All promised assistance. *Promises not kept,* I thought.

Suddenly exhaustion overwhelmed me. I was tired from battling Jayden and Lady Azura and most of all,

Marco. I sank into Lady Azura's big armchair. I couldn't stop Marco, yet he was intent on stopping me. He'd thrown a ball at me today. Who knew what tomorrow would bring? I had a feeling it would only get worse until he got what he wanted—me gone.

The teacup used to read Jayden's leaves rested on the table before me. I leaned closer. I searched for the guitar shape that Lady Azura had seen. All I saw were blobs of dried out tea leaves. There was no point searching for answers here, I realized. I had to do something. Stop this myself.

Then I saw Lady Azura's crystal bell, and it was as if a bell chimed inside my head. I knew what I had to do.

Lady Azura used the bell to call spirits to her.

I'd never done it before, but I was going to try. I'd bring Marco here, to me, now and have it out with him. Set boundaries. *Command* him to go.

I grabbed the crystal bell and rang it to the four corners of the earth the way Lady Azura did. Calling Marco's name. Meditating on him. Drawing him out.

Would it work?

Chapter 12

Nothing happened. I sat alone in a room of astrological charts and tarot cards. The one time I wanted to see the dead, and I couldn't.

I'd watched Lady Azura summon the dead with this bell. She rang it four times and . . . what? I closed my eyes, trying to recall. She'd touched the hands of the person who'd come to see her to connect with the spirit.

But Jayden wasn't here.

I opened my eyes and spotted the tea cup. The cup with Jayden's tea leaves. I plunged two fingers into the remains. It was worth a try. I rang the cut-crystal bell, intoning the chant.

I willed my body to relax and my mind to go blank.

"MarcoMarcoMarcoMarco." His name ran together as I repeated it.

My stomach contracted as a wave of nausea overtook me.

"Marco. Marco." Something was happening.

Sweat beaded along my hairline. The stomach pains grew stronger.

And then he was there. Marco. Shimmering before me. Hoodie and shorts. Bare feet hovering centimeters above the floor. Scowling.

I was so amazed, I nearly whooped with joy. I'd done it! I'd actually summoned a spirit.

Marco began to fade. I refocused my energy on him and only him. Bringing him back.

My joy quickly transformed to fear as I realized what I'd done. I'd brought Marco here to me. I was alone with a spirit who hated me.

Now what?

The spot behind my eyes began to throb. My stomach felt as if a fist were grabbing it and wringing it like a sponge.

"Why?" I managed to croak. "Why are you doing this to me?"

Marco didn't speak. He just glared.

The room swayed. The turkey sandwich from

lunch so many hours ago threatened to come back up.

Marco moved toward me. Closer and closer.

I pushed back against the chair's nubby fabric. Nowhere to go. No escape.

He reached out, and I cringed as his hand touched my shoulder. A current jolted through my body, forcing every hair to stand on end.

The light grew brighter. Brighter. The glare of the sun caused me to shade my eyes.

I peered at Marco over the expanse of the rocky ledge.

Back on the ledge above the river. Back with Marco and his friends outside in the summer sun.

A girl with auburn braids wordlessly handed me a pair of aviator sunglasses. I put them on and mouthed, *Thanks*. Then I watched Marco.

Alive. In color. Laughing with the blond-haired girl.

"Come out with me tonight," he told her.

"I have plans." She giggled and leaned back on her pink towel.

"With me," Marco insisted. His eyes were nut brown. Deep, warm eyes like Jayden's. "Come on, you have to say yes sometime."

"Maybe sometime," the girl teased. She batted her long lashes at him. "You need to prove you like me."

"Anything," Marco said.

"Go swimming in the river," she said.

"Easy," Marco scoffed. He stood, wearing the dark hoodie and board shorts he'd wear for eternity. He headed for the dirt path that wound through the pines toward the riverbed.

"No, that's not what I meant. I want you to jump!" the girl called.

"Jump?" Marco gazed over the side of the ledge. I scuttled across my towel to get a better view. The swirling river waters looked a long way down.

"Yeah." The girl stood next to him now. "Jimmy did it last week, didn't you, Jimmy?"

The boy on the nearby towel nodded. "It's a wicked jump. Major splash. But you got to aim it right. Got to hit the deep spot in the middle."

Marco furrowed his brow, assessing the jump. He didn't look convinced. "Water's too cold to jump today. Besides, I'm late to get my little bro."

"Don't be such a chicken," the girl teased. She giggled and flapped her skinny arms in an imitation of a chicken.

Marco stood straighter. "Do not call me that."

"Then do it. Do it for me," the girl wheedled.

Marco glanced down again and then at the girl. He really liked this girl. I could see the spell she cast reflected in his eyes.

"I dare you," she coaxed.

Marco didn't answer. He just walked to the edge of the rock, and without even taking off his hoodie, cannonballed over the edge.

We all heard the splash.

I scrambled to the edge so fast I scraped my knees. Everyone hurried around me. The dark blue waters swirled, throwing up white foam around the many small rocks.

Searching. Searching. We were all searching the water.

Where was he? I looked frantically for Marco's head.

"Could he be underwater for this long?" one girl asked.

"I bet he's trying to scare us," Jimmy said.

"I didn't think he'd really do it," the girl who'd dared him murmured. Her face seemed to have lost its tan.

The tears streamed down my cheeks. Hot tears. Tears of grief. It would take his friends several minutes more to discover that Marco wasn't playing tricks. Marco wasn't ever going to surface.

This was how Marco had died.

A swimming accident.

Caused by a stupid dare.

"Marco!" the blond girl shrieked next to me. Anguish filled her voice. As the others raced down the path toward the water, she rocked in place, her tears flowing as fast as mine.

I lifted my hand to wipe my dripping nose and inhaled the pungent odor of strong tea.

Tea. I pulled my hand back. Thick, black tea leaves stuck to my finger.

I gazed around. Dimness. The sunlight gone. I was in Lady Azura's room. Marco—a shadow of the vibrant boy he'd once been—hovered before me.

"I'm so sorry," I whispered. What else could I say? His death was senseless.

Then, for the first time, Marco spoke to me.

"Stay away from my brother. You are trouble."

Chapter 13

I sat by myself on the porch swing.

Not totally by myself. I was with the spirit that knits. She worked her needles, paying no attention to me or the neighbors entering the house.

I liked her. She did her own thing and left me alone.

I knew I should be inside. The party had started an hour ago. Lady Azura already had a line for quick palm readings. Kids and adults were drinking soda with fake eyeball ice cubes and eating cookies shaped like bones.

It was just pre-Halloween fun, but this year it seemed wrong. Disrespectful. Death wasn't a joke. Ever since Marco showed me what had happened, I couldn't stop thinking about him and what he'd said about me.

He'd said I was trouble. What kind of trouble?

The question kept me up at night. I would never hurt Jayden. Never.

The moon was full in the dark sky. The blue moon. I glanced at Knitting Woman. Was the blue moon affecting her? Was she knitting faster?

The rising notes of a creepy melody floated from the house. I shivered and wrapped my arms around myself. The cold air smelled of danger. Something was about to happen. Every nerve in my body told me so. Brittle leaves rustled as the wind swept through the branches. White figures fluttered from the tree across the street.

Toilet paper, I knew. I'd seen two of Lily's brothers draping the neighborhood trees earlier.

A faint but insistent tapping echoed from above. The spirit of the sailor rattled the tall windows. All the spirits inside were agitated. The man with the mustache paced the second floor, emphasizing each step. If the music and chatter hadn't been so loud downstairs, everyone could have heard the creaking of the old floorboards.

Lily, Tamara, and Miranda were inside. Dad had run out to get pizza, but he'd be back soon. The streetlights illuminated sections of the dark pavement. I glimpsed Lily's aunt Angela heading toward our house with a tall man I guessed was her husband. I peered past her into the darkness. Still waiting. Hoping.

Jayden hadn't shown up.

"Sara!" Angela wore black skinny jeans and high heels, and her dark hair fell in waves all the way down her back. "Take us inside." She reached for my hand.

I walked them into the house. The front sitting room was packed with people. Others lined up outside Lady Azura's velvet curtain, waiting for their glimpse of the future.

"Oh, I love it!" Angela squealed. "Robby, do you hear those moans? So spooky!"

And so real, I thought.

The spirit's pacing had grown more frantic upstairs. *Pound, pound, pound.* His steps synched with the beating of my heart.

Bad, bad, the voice repeated in my head. *This is bad.* But what could I do? I couldn't kick all these people out, and I couldn't hide on the porch all night.

"Wild, right?" Lily slid beside me. Her eyelids glittered with a sparkly silver shadow. She wore a black sequined top. I'd gone to the opposite extreme. Bright pink and green. Anti-scary. Anti-death.

"Who are all these people?" I asked.

"See, advertising works!" She grinned. "Listen, it's too crazy down here. I sent the group to the third floor to hang out. Let's bring food up."

"The third floor?" I squeaked in disbelief. She couldn't have!

"Your craft room. There's way more room up there. Plus, there are too many old people down here. I turned off all the lights and just flicked on the twinkly ones around the window. Great vibe." Lily reached for a bowl of chips.

Bad, bad, rapped my internal DJ. I had to get everyone back downstairs. I followed Lily in a daze as we climbed to my craft room. What would I find?

Miranda, Tamara, Marlee, Luke, Garrett, both Jacks, and two girls whose names I wasn't sure of were hanging out. I stole a glance at the closet door. Still shut. I crossed my fingers that Henry stayed inside.

"Maybe we should go back—" I started.

Lily wouldn't hear of it. "This is the perfect spot for ghost stories. I can scare everyone!"

Lily had the boys push the large table to one side and close the door. We sat on the floor in a circle. I sat too. I wasn't going downstairs by myself. Maybe if I stayed here nothing weird would happen, I reasoned. This made no sense, I knew, but I couldn't think straight.

Maybe the moon was getting to me, too.

I sat between Tamara and Luke, but I could barely make out their faces in the darkness. I gnawed the hangnail on my thumb and stared at the closet door, scarcely listening to Lily's story. If it opened, I'd jump into action, I decided. I'd scream fire or something and get everyone out.

"He traveled down the wet, wet highway, feeling as if someone were watching him. He glanced into the rear-view mirror and checked the backseat. He was alone. He turned off the highway, starting down a deserted side road. . . ." Lily spoke in an eerie monotone.

I shivered. Not from the story.

"And he approached a crossroads. A woman appeared on the road in front of his car. He slammed on the brakes, praying he wouldn't hit her. The car stopped and he looked around for the woman. . . ."

The creaking of floorboards. I strained my ears,

listening to ghostly footsteps. Footsteps only I could hear.

"And then her face pressed against his window. Her eyes glowed red. Her pointy teeth dripped saliva. . . ."

The footsteps drew closer. Up the stairs. Heading toward us. I watched the closet door. Could it be?

"Her clawed hand grabbed the door handle. She pulled, rattling the car. He screamed as the door—"

The door swung open. Not the closet door, but the door to the room. I whirled around. Had Henry gotten out of the closet?

A shadow filled the doorway.

Tamara gasped. So did another girl. They saw him too!

I dug my fingernails into my palms and waited for them to scream.

"What's with circle time in the dark?" the shadow asked. He stepped into the room.

"Jayden! You made it!" Jack L. cheered.

I stared. Not a spirit. Jayden.

"I thought you weren't coming," Lily said.

"I wasn't." Jayden never looked at me. Maybe he didn't see me in the dark. "Your aunt Angela convinced my mom to come. Mom dragged me and my dad. So here I am."

I remembered Angela once saying she lived near Jayden's family. I hadn't known she and his mom were friends. Jayden didn't look unhappy to be here. That was good.

He peered around the circle the best he could in the light of the small blinking bulbs. "What are you doing?" He scanned the group without stopping at me. Purposely not looking at me.

"Scary stories." Tamara scooted to her right, pushing against Lily with her thigh. "Sit here," she commanded.

Jayden hesitated, and my muscles stiffened. Would he refuse to sit next to me?

Everyone waited. He had no choice. He lowered himself into the small space between me and Tamara.

He smelled wonderfully like Jayden. I kept my eyes on the closet door, content for now to just be near him.

Lily started a new story. Something about a headless horseman. I couldn't concentrate with Jayden so close.

So close. What would Marco do?

I stole a sideways glance. Confused, I twisted my

head about. I couldn't see him, but more important, I couldn't feel him. Marco wasn't here.

Had he left? I'd never seen him not by Jayden's side. My minded sorted through the possibilities. Had Jayden discovered Marco? Could Lady Azura have stopped Marco?

Jayden leaned anxiously toward the open door to the hall. The pale light and muffled voices from downstairs filtered up.

"You okay?" I whispered.

"No." He sounded angry. Maybe scared.

I shot him a questioning look.

"Lady Azura took my parents in to give them a reading," he whispered over Lily's storytelling. "Lily's aunt's brilliant idea."

That explained it. There was no way Marco was missing that. He was downstairs.

Then it hit me. I was alone with Jayden for the very first time. Alone with ten other kids but no Marco.

Lily spoke on. As I sat next to Jayden, trying to think of what to say, I heard the whispers to my left.

"When are we going to Dina's?"

"Dina keeps texting me. She wants us to come over now."

"So can we leave yet?"

Part of me was happy. I wanted everyone to clear out and go to Dina's, so I could hide under a comforter and deal the way I always had with the dead creaking about. Then I thought of Lily and Lady Azura. They'd talked of nothing but this party for days. If everyone left, they'd be so sad.

I glanced at Jayden. Would he go to Dina's too?

Spots of lights began to dance before my eyes. I tensed. Was Marco back? I sometimes saw spots before the spirits came.

"What's with the lights?" Tamara whispered.

"So spooky!" Miranda gave a witchlike cackle for effect.

The Christmas lights sputtered, no longer blinking rhythmically. The closet door swung on its hinges. Back and forth, as if being pulled by an invisible string.

Or hand.

I saw Henry's hand. As I stared frozen in horror, Henry's full body materialized. He scampered about, clearly excited by such a captive audience. In seconds he was at the bookcase behind me. He lifted an over-size photography book high above his head. But no one else saw him. They all just saw a huge book float-ing toward the ceiling.

"D-do you see that?" Marlee's voice shook.

"Wicked cool," Garrett whispered.

Everyone watched in wide-eyed wonder.

Henry dropped the book, and it smashed against the floor. Then he grabbed three small paint containers. Red, yellow, orange. Up and around the paint pots flew as he juggled them. Joy radiated from his slight form as every-one sucked in their breath, staring at the swirling colors in mute fascination.

For now.

Soon it would unravel before my eyes——my new friends freaking out, terrified of my haunted house, real-izing I could see the ghosts, laughing and whispering about me in school.

No! screamed a voice in my head. *You can't let that happen.*

Before I knew it I was standing. "My dad rigged this all up. Did it scare you?" My voice rang out with a confi-dence I didn't know I had.

"Oh, wow, so much!" Lily breathed, as the floating paint pots dropped to the floor.

"I was never scared," Luke boasted.

Marlee looked terrified but nodded in shaky agreement.

"How did he do that?" Jayden asked as he stood. "I don't see any wires."

"I promised never to reveal his special effects secrets," I said.

Everyone was talking at once. Not scared, but amazed. Now no one whispered about leaving.

Henry leaned against the bookcase, smirking.

"There's, uh, pizza downstairs. We should eat it while it's hot." I tried to lead them toward the door.

But no one moved. In fact, Lily had everyone sit again for more spooky stories. Nothing I said could convince them. After the supernatural jolt from the floating objects, they were more intent than ever on scaring one another.

I couldn't sit. I couldn't stand still. I balanced on the balls of my feet, eyeing Henry, my heart hammering. Henry turned toward the corner, his back to me. What was he doing? When he moved toward the circle, I moved too.

"Sara, sit down," Miranda said. "You're ruining the mood."

I couldn't. Henry's form shimmered with an unearthly glow. He moved like a cat in search of prey. Here one moment, across the room the next. His dark eyes gleamed, calculating where to strike.

My heart pounded even louder. I didn't know what to do.

Henry paused before Tamara. She sat cross-legged, listening to Luke describe a flesh-eating zombie, totally unaware of the big spider Henry held. Its long, thin legs kicked the air as Henry lowered it toward Tamara's reddish-brown waves. Her hair would soon be a nest for an enormous spider!

I lunged toward them, pushing Henry, but there was nothing to push. My arms sliced through the air. My body propelled forward, leaving me splayed on my hands and knees.

"What the—?" Tamara stared in astonishment, as I lay on the floor next to her, having seemingly launched myself from across the room. I couldn't explain. There was no time.

Henry was laughing.

Laughing at me.

At my friends.

I scrambled to my feet. I had to stop him. The spider scurried across the floor unseen, back to its corner. Henry ran about the room, tossing things as he went. Chips, napkins, Garrett's cell phone. I raced after him, not thinking about how crazy I looked.

He dodged to the left and right, always just out of reach, giggling like a little boy. But I was fast. I backed him up against the wall. I tried to calm my rasping breaths so I could focus. Focus on Henry.

Stop. Stop, I tried to command him with my mind.

Henry smirked at my lame attempt. Then, with surprising strength, he pushed the heavy wooden bookcase. As if in slow motion, I watched the bookcase rock and then tip, heading for Jayden, who sat with his back turned.

"No!" I screamed. I threw myself at Jayden.

My hands pushed his shoulder. He moved with more ease than I'd expected. I stared at Jayden's shirt. At my hands and at the pair of hands next to mine.

There were two of us, pushing him out of danger.

Chapter 14

Jayden tumbled to his side. The heavy bookcase banged to the floor, narrowly missing him. Fear and confusion flashed across his face.

Anger like I'd never felt filled my head, making it hard to think. If that bookcase had fallen on Jayden, he would have been seriously hurt. My body shook with emotion. All I could think about was getting this spirit out of my room and away from my friends.

"No!" I screamed again. My anger mixed with terror at the realization of what Henry could do. "Stop it! Stop it now!" I pushed my face close to Henry's undulating form. "Go away!"

Henry gave a slight whimper, then began to fade. The closet door creaked eerily on its hinges as it closed.

Gone. He was gone.

I did it, I thought. *I was strong. I got rid of him.* I wanted to be happy, but I felt numb. The room was silent. Everyone stared at me. I examined my shoelaces, too exhausted to create another lie.

"Are you okay?" Lily hurried to my side.

"Yeah. Those ghost stories got to me." I shot her a pleading look.

She didn't miss a beat. "Zombies freak me out too. When that bookcase tumbled, I totally thought it was a zombie."

"I told you it was an excellent story!" Luke beamed.

"But Sara was running all around," Marlee murmured. "The chips were—"

She didn't get to finish. My father burst through the door, Lily's mother and aunt right behind him. "What happened? Is everyone all right? We heard a crash!" Dad flicked on the light switch.

"The bookcase fell," Lily explained. She squinted in the sudden brightness.

"Awesome special effects, Mr. Collins!" Garrett exclaimed. He moved close to my dad. "Seriously, I've got to know how you did it."

Dad raised his eyebrows at me.

I shrugged and forced my biggest smile.

Garrett talked on, telling my dad about his dream to go to Hollywood and do special effects for the movies. Dad just nodded.

Mrs. Randazzo surveyed the mess. "You kids did enough damage up here. Time to get downstairs for pizza."

"But—" Miranda began.

"No buts," Lily's mom replied. "Downstairs. Now. All of you."

Unlike with me, everyone listened to her. Lily led the way to the kitchen.

"I'm just going to clean up a bit," I told Dad. He lingered in the doorway with Garrett, who now described the special effects he'd designed on the computer.

"Fine, don't be long." Dad clapped a hand on Garrett's back to move him forward. "We can discuss this over pizza." They headed toward the kitchen.

I turned to face the empty room. I'd come really close to disaster, but I'd done what Lady Azura had told me to do. I'd asserted myself and made Henry go away.

Then I realized that the room wasn't empty.

"I'll help." His voice was soft. He held some of the books that had nearly clobbered him. Jayden had stayed behind.

And so had Marco.

Marco shimmered beside his brother.

I remembered the hands. The hands beside mine. They were Marco's. Marco had appeared to keep Jayden from danger.

Danger caused by me.

The realization made my legs weak.

"Thank you." Jayden's voice jolted me. "If you hadn't gone for the dive tackle, that bookcase would've pancaked me."

"You're welcome." I wasn't sure what else to say. I felt calmer than I'd ever felt near him. The nervous, fluttery feeling was gone. "I'm glad you came, even though I guess this party isn't so great."

"You're wrong. It's fun." He grinned. "And dangerous."

"It is Mischief Night," I said, returning his smile. "A blue moon, too."

Together we righted the bookcase and replaced the books. "I shouldn't have yelled like that the other day."

"It's okay," I said. I picked up the paint pots. Luckily,

the lids had stayed tight. "I was butting in. I need to mind my own—"

"No, you don't," Jayden said quickly. "It's nice you care. I mean, it's nice to talk to someone about it. To you, about it." He seemed embarrassed.

"You must really miss your brother." I spoke to Marco now as much as Jayden. "I can tell that he meant a lot to you."

Jayden nodded and leaned against the table. "I do. We all do. My mom . . . she was wrecked when Marco died. She couldn't bear to live in our house without him. That's why we moved up here." He brushed off some potato chip crumbs. "She thought leaving would help, but it didn't. Now she's up here alone and the rest of our family is still down in Atlanta."

"That must be rough for her," I said. "And lonely."

Jayden nodded. "She worries, too. About me. A lot." He paused. "It hurts her so much that Marco is gone."

"He's not, though," I said softly. "He's always with you."

"Yeah, I know," he scoffed. "People say that all the time. That his memory lives on and all."

"No, really." I eyed Marco. He stood, listening, but strangely, for once, did not come between us. "Your brother still watches over you. Don't ask me how I know, but I do. He's there for you when you need him."

Jayden rolled his eyes "I've heard that before. You know, I've never told anyone this, but I actually hope he's not. I hope Marco's soul, spirit, whatever, is far, far away from here. On a tropical beach. He loved the beach. It sounds horrible, but we need to be free of him."

"But maybe he's here to help you," I offered.

"Maybe." Jayden was silent for a moment. "But he's crushing us, and that's not helping. That's what I was trying to tell Lady Azura. I've been trying to tell my mom, too."

"And?"

"She didn't want to hear it at first, but lately . . ." He shrugged. "Maybe Lady Azura can help. That's why I left them downstairs with her."

I kept my gaze on Marco. His shoulders had slumped. He no longer looked defiant.

Jayden's eyes suddenly widened. "Oh, wow, I'm sorry. Your mom died too, right?"

"Yeah. But that's okay. I mean, I can still talk about this with you."

"Do you ever feel"—he scratched his head trying to find the words—"that she's still here too?"

I found it hard to swallow. My eyes darted from Marco to the closed closet door where Henry was. I saw spirits everywhere, yet I'd never seen my mother. "No," I admitted. "And that really stinks."

"But maybe that's better."

"I don't know." And I didn't. I'd been so sure that Marco was bad news, but I'd give anything for a glimpse of my mother.

"Okay, too much downer talk. Time for a channel change," Jayden said. "Want to come trick-or-treating tomorrow? A bunch of us are going."

I looked to Marco, waiting for him to stop me.

He remained silent. Not moving. Defeated.

"Sure," I said to Jayden. "I'd like that."

When we got downstairs, Jayden took off in search of his parents. I found Dad still serving pizza.

"Sara." He waved me over. "There's someone I'd like you to meet."

A tall woman with shoulder-length dark hair and

cat's-eye glasses stood next to him. The new girl-friend. "This is Janelle."

She smiled and greeted me. We talked about the party, commenting on how most people had opted to dress in black. She seemed nice enough.

"You'll have to come to my house later and meet my daughter. I wanted her to come tonight, but she's getting ready for her party. She's having one tonight too," she said.

"Really?" I scanned the room for Lily. I had to tell her about trick-or-treating with Jayden.

"She goes to your school, although I think you're younger. Right, Mike?"

My dad shrugged. "Sara's in seventh grade. Your daughter's in—"

"Eighth. I'm sure that's why Sara didn't know about her party." Janelle turned to me. "Her name's Dina."

That got my attention. My dad was dating Dina Martino's mother!

Great. Just great.

"Excuse me. I'm going to find more napkins," I said. I had to process this news. Lily was never going to believe it. What were the chances?

I slipped into the pantry just outside the kitchen and closed the door so only a sliver of the party sounds filtered in. I needed quiet for a minute. There was so much to think about.

But I wasn't alone in the pantry.

Marco was there.

Arms folded, he moved toward me, pushing me back against the shelves.

"Go away," I hissed. I had to be firm. I'd learned that tonight. "I don't want you here."

"You can't tell me what to do." His voice was low and measured. "I'm not like that little boy."

Now what? I thought, panicked. My fingers found my necklace and rubbed the hematite.

Boundaries.

"You can stop that." He nodded at my hand clutching the hematite. "I am not here to hurt you."

We stood in silence. The noise of the party seemed miles away, yet I could hear Jayden's voice. He must be near.

"Why did you call me trouble?" I finally asked.

"For one thing, you can see me."

"Why is that bad?" I kept my voice low.

"You attract others like me. You attract trouble."
He raised his chin toward the ceiling.

I knew what he meant. Henry.

Lily brought him out, I wanted to say. But I was
the one who saw him and chased him. Because of
me, the bookcase got pushed.

"I died because I did something stupid for a girl I
liked," he said.

"I know," I whispered. "I saw."

"And I hurt my family. I can't let Jayden make the
same mistake. Around you, the chances of him doing
something stupid are high."

"But I won't let him! I'm not like that."

"I saw that. You saved him. You got to him before
me." Marco backed away, and his voice choked. "He
doesn't want me anymore."

"He's growing up," I said. "He needs space."

"I was supposed to babysit him that day."

"He doesn't need a babysitter anymore."

Marco didn't speak or move for the longest time.
My words floated in the air between us. He knew it
was time to move on. I could sense how much it hurt
him to leave.

"He was lucky to have you, you know." I thought about my dad out there with his new girlfriend, about all the spirits haunting this house, about facing mean Dina at school, about trying to hide what I could do from my friends. "Some of us could use a guardian angel."

"What makes you think you don't have one?" he asked.

"Who . . . ?" I didn't finish. *My mom?* Was my mom watching over me? "Is my mom here? I can't see her. Can you see her, Marco?"

Marco just shook his head. "You still have a lot to learn about yourself." He opened the pantry door with his bare foot. "Worry less about the spirits you can and can't see, and more about the living. Find out who you are. There are many ways to open your eyes."

"Open my eyes?" What did he mean?

But Marco was gone.

I peeked out the door into the house still filled with people. Jayden shared a laugh with his parents in the hall. Lily's aunt talked with my dad and Dina's mom in the kitchen. I joined Lily, Tamara, and Miranda on the long line outside the velvet curtain.

"Lady Azura is rocking it tonight," Lily confided, pulling me close to them.

"I can't wait to talk to her," Tamara said. "I have so many questions."

So did I, I realized. I thought back to that day at the arcade, after the boardwalk closed. I'd been unhappy with all the change. Now, I realized, it was me who needed to change. No more hiding. I had to find out exactly who I was and what I could do.

I crossed my fingers that I'd like what I'd find.

Want to know what happens to Sara next?

Here's a sneak peek at the next book in the series:

Spirits
of the
Season

I laughed the kind of laughter that takes over your body and makes you feel as if you have to pee.

"Do you dare me to wear this to school?" Lily Randazzo teased. She posed with one hand on her hip, as if she was being photographed for a fashion magazine. But no fashion magazine would feature the ridiculous frilly patchwork apron or the silly knit cap covered with dozens of green and red pom-poms she was wearing.

"You would never," I said, still laughing. "It goes beyond all acceptable ugly."

"That's what makes the combo so great," Lily said, pulling off the hat and apron and placing them back on the store's table. "It's so repulsive that it crosses that line into cool." She eyed them again. "Or not."

"Not," I agreed. I'd already decided to come back later and buy the ugly hat for Lily. She'd laugh on Christmas morning when she opened it. Our inside joke.

I had a best friend and inside jokes. Unbelievable. Everything was so different here in Stellamar.

Better.

"Sara, what am I possibly going to buy here?" Lily whispered. She pulled out a piece of notebook paper scribbled with a list of at least thirty names. "I have to get gifts for all these cousins. Everyone comes to our house on Christmas Eve. A cozy dinner for sixty. Mom started cooking last summer!"

I tucked my long blond hair behind my ears and stared at Lily's list. She had more relatives in and around this tiny town than the town library had books. Or so it seemed. Of course, our town was really small and so was its library, but she still had *a lot*.

"My whole list can fit on a Post-It note," I said. "Dad and Lady Azura. That's it."

But two was more than one, I knew. Way more. Until recently, it would've only been Dad on my list.

I glanced around the store, the Salty Crab, owned

by Lily's aunt Delores. It was a mystery how this woman was related to Lily. Lily had style. She wore cute outfits, oversize sunglasses, and lots of silver jewelry. The Salty Crab sold dresses that could double as tablecloths, sweaters with holiday themes, candles in the shapes of elves and reindeer, and lots of chunky plastic necklaces.

"We could walk somewhere else," I suggested, pointing out the window to Beach Drive.

Lily picked up a snow globe of the Stellamar boardwalk. "My mom says I have to get some stuff here. Family pity. What about you?" She pointed to a nearby display. "Tie with a huge Santa face for your dad?"

"Going to pass on that," I said. "I'm making my gifts. For Dad, I'm decorating a wooden box with some tiny shells I found on the beach."

"You're so good with crafty things," Lily said. "What about Lady Azura?"

"I don't know," I confided. "I want to make her something too, but it has to be special. You know?"

"Totally one-of-a-kind," Lily agreed. "Nobody else is like her."

I watched the tiny snowflakes fall inside the glass

ball as Lily shook it. After four months of sharing a house with the old woman, I still didn't know a lot about her. Nothing personal. But I did know we had a connection. We saw things the same way.

A way I couldn't even begin to explain to Lily.

A way no one else could imagine.

About the Author

Phoebe Rivers had a brush with the paranormal when she was thirteen years old, and ever since then she has been fascinated by people who see spirits and can communicate with them. In addition to her intrigue with all things paranormal, Phoebe also loves cats, French cuisine, and writing stories. She has written dozens of books for children of all ages and is thrilled to now be exploring Sara's paranormal world.